WHEN ANGELS CRY

D0439455

WHEN ANGELS CRY

A Novel

JENNIFER EDWARDS

YUCCA

Yucca Publishing books may be purchased in bulk at special discounts for sales promotion, corporate gifts, fund-raising, or educational purposes. Special editions can also be created to specifications. For details, contact the Special Sales Department, Yucca Publishing, 307 West 36th Street, 11th Floor, New York, NY 10018 or yucca@skyhorsepublishing.com.

Yucca Publishing® is an imprint of Skyhorse Publishing, Inc.®, a Delaware corporation.

Visit our website at www.yuccapub.com.

10 9 8 7 6 5 4 3 2 1

Library of Congress Cataloging-in-Publication Data is available on file.

Cover design by Yucca Publishing

Print ISBN: 978-1-63158-006-2
Ebook ISBN: 978-1-63158-038-3

Printed in the United States of America

Chapter One

If This Is Hell . . .
It Must Be My Mother's House

It's funny it hadn't occurred to me until that very moment, when I pulled into my mother's driveway, that the idea of losing her would devastate me more than I could have ever imagined. There were times I had wished the pills that she'd swallowed had taken effect or other times when she drove me so far round the twist that I imagined my hands squeezing the life from her. Now, as the prospect of her mortality looms, I already feel a tremendous sense of loss. As I stare at the house that I used to dread coming home to, I am feeling things I never thought possible.

To begin with, the house itself seemed smaller to me. It had always seemed to stand quite proudly. A lovely Cape Cod. But now the white paint seemed dull, and the hunter green shutters looked more the color of pea soup. Stepping out of my trusty Prius, the familiar crunch of pebbles under my shoes welcomed me. When I was seven, I rode my Schwinn with the butterfly handlebars up this driveway at full speed, then hit the brakes, skidding for the last few feet and sending up dust and tiny rocks into the air. The sound it made was exhilarating, and it never failed to annoy my mother.

"Sarah! Stop doing that out there!" she would yell. "You're behaving like a hoodlum!"

Whatever hoodlum meant, I knew, at that moment, I wanted to be one.

I walked around to the trunk and opened it, revealing the lovely, and oh so sturdy, black Tumi suitcase set my husband had bought me the year before. I should have known there was nothing subtle about the gift. He might not even have been aware of it at the time. The bottom line was that he wanted me to "pack up" and leave, but he was too much of a coward to tell me. He made my life unbearable, until I finally did pack up the unused luggage, and moved out. He has since been playing house with a twenty-seven-year-old assistant from his office, typical right? And now I am about to move back in with my seventy-year-old angry, resentful, delusional mother . . . oh joy!

"Sarah . . . that you?" My mother called from behind the front door screen. She had always had a lovely speaking voice. Similar to Lauren Bacall. Lately she sounded like an ex-two-pack-a-day smoker.

"Yes Ma . . . it's me," I said as I picked up the last piece of my expensive luggage, trying to balance them all. My agent said I always carried the weight of the world around. Maybe I needed a personal skycap! I could use one just to deal with all the "emotional" baggage I seem to be carrying these days.

The screen door flung open. "Oh . . . my darling Sarah. You're home!" With that, my mother actually seemed to be running towards me. Out onto the porch, down numerous stairs. I didn't trust what I was actually seeing. She was moving at quite a clip despite the fact she had her hip replaced. How could she be running so fast? And should she be running so fast? She was at my side in record time. And to make matters worse, she was wearing a bubble gum pink jogging suit.

"Hello, Mother," I said, trying not to look too dazed and confused.

"Put your bags upstairs and let's go for a run!" She began prancing in place like my pretty pony.

All the bags I was holding were causing me to lose feeling in the lower half of my body. I wanted to S.O.S. my therapist, in hopes that he would somehow be able to navigate my next move. But I am a grown forty-five-year-old woman. It's time to make decisions on my own.

"Mother . . . I don't run," I said defiantly. "You know that. But I will put my bags down and maybe have a cup of tea . . . or vodka. I've been driving for eight hours. You know how long it takes from Los Angeles to Marin?"

"Oh, honey, of course you have . . . How thoughtless of me! Go to your room, settle down, and when I get back, I'll make peanut butter and jelly sandwiches!" Launching herself forward like Jackie Joyner at the Olympics, my mother took off running down the long driveway, veering right and disappearing behind the six-foot hedge in front of the house.

I watched dumbfounded for a while to see if she might reappear. Nope. So I lugged my Tumi's up the porch steps and into the front hallway of the house I grew up in.

At first sight, everything seemed about the same as it always had. The dark, hardwood floors had lost their luster a long time ago. Looking into the living room on my left, I could tell that the framed photos on top of the baby grand were arranged as they had been for decades.

My mother always made sure that the photographs of family members, dead or alive, were positioned correctly, and the frames, dust free and brightly polished. The couch and love seat were fairly new. My mother was going through a gingham stage and had bought two red and white checkered pieces. They reminded me of tablecloths used in pizzerias. All that was missing was a bottle of Chianti . . . The new furniture was not my cup of Chian-Tea!

I began my ascent up the staircase struck by the number of photographs lining the wall from the bottom of the stairs to the second floor. I think maybe four generations of O'Malley's were there and all the Mancuso's. Half of these people meant nothing to me. All through my childhood whenever I asked about a family member, my mother and father would become inexplicably mute. I never understood what they could be hiding or avoiding. I remember sitting in the middle of the staircase, at a very early age, and staring at certain photos on the wall wondering if the stories I had heard were true. One of the smaller photos was of a pretty young girl. She was four years old in this picture. So delicate, petite. Her hair was an explosion of blonde ringlets. She seemed to be perfect in almost every way.

Rachel, my younger sister, was the apple of my parents' eye, and a favorite of everyone else she was around. Rachel seemed to glow from within. Even though we were only two years apart, she was miles ahead of me. Talking before she could walk, making friends with anyone and everyone . . . she was my parents' pride and joy. She was mine, too.

I don't know how long I stood in the stairwell looking at the family photos, but as I climbed the stairs, I caught the photo I had tried to avoid my whole life. A photo of the exquisite Rachel. The child who would "go somewhere." A child who was everything that Olivia and Jack O'Malley wanted . . . the child who was supposed to carry on the family traditions and make them proud. It was an extraordinary photo of a six-year-old, ringlet haired, girl in a cherry wood coffin. Why they had her photographed like this I never understood. Even more puzzling was why this haunting image of her corpse adorned our walls.

Once upstairs, I walked into the bedroom I had shared with Rachel.

It had been converted into an office. Every book that my father had owned lined the bookshelves on three sides of the room. In the event of an earthquake anyone lying on the sofa bed would be squashed by literature. The room still smelled of my father. Though he had been dead a few years, his scent somehow lingered. In the leather chair, in the curtains, in the books. I set my cases down and sat on the sofa bed, convinced I should have stayed in a motel. I suddenly felt so weary. I always enjoyed the drive up the coast, but my body didn't like being stationary for too long anymore. The Pacific Coast Highway had been the only way I liked to head North. Driving so close to the ocean quieted my mind.

Over the years, when I was depressed or just needed to think, I would drive to the beach, listen to the waves, and feel connected again. Sometimes when I stay in a hotel for any length of time, I bring my sound machine that mimics the ocean. And I sleep like a baby.

I have always had a thing for pelicans. They remind me of what dinosaurs must have looked like. And the brilliance of their feeding technique was awesome. Watching them fold their entire bodies up into feathered spears and piercing the water with such force still blows my mind.

Today the pelicans seemed to put on a special show just for me! I saw hundreds, in their V-formations gliding above my car. It was as if they were leading me toward my destination. At least I liked to think that they were.

I curled up on the sofa and shut my eyes. It hadn't been more than thirty minutes when I heard a sound that reminded me of something I had heard on Animal Planet. I believe it was the cry of a wildebeest in heat. I heard it again. A piercing howl. This time I recognized the alarming noise came from my mother. My feet barely touched the ground as I flew down the stairs and out the back door to find the source of the terrifying sound. I stopped in my tracks. Standing in our back yard was a large airstream trailer with the sun reflecting off its shiny surface. It resembled a space ship. A man stood buck-naked in the doorway of the alien craft. I do believe the gentleman was Manuel Hernandez. Mother had told us he was her gardener. Maybe this will make sense in the next couple of minutes . . . . Maybe not.

The image of what happened next will go with me to my grave. My mother, Olivia Rose Mancuso O'Malley appeared in the buff behind Manuel Hernandez and put her arms around his waist. As Manuel turned to face her, she kissed him on the mouth, and he slapped her on her seventy-year-old buttocks. She made that weird noise again. I realized that it was in fun and that she obviously wasn't being dismembered as I had imagined upon waking. I closed the back door without her noticing and headed for the freezer. There was always a bottle of vodka in my parent's freezer. We sometimes went without milk for days, but a bottle of vodka, of varying degrees of quality, and quantity, was always found right next to the ice cream.

Within moments of my finding the martini olives, my mother burst into the kitchen in her glow-in-the-dark jogging suit. "Hello Sarah," she said, out of breath.

"Did you have a good run Mother?" I emphasized the word run.

"Oh, yes," she said as she reached for the vodka. "And a terrific fuck, too!" She plonked an olive in her glass as I stood mouth agape.

"What's wrong, sweetie? You look like you swallowed a lemon!"

Words formed in my brain, but I was unable to speak.

"Well, if you're going to act like a mute, I'm going to take a quick shower!" My mother downed her vodka in one shot and left me standing in the kitchen.

I don't think I ever heard my mother use the "F" word, let alone do the "F" thing! My brother Henry had told me that she had gone bonkers and was in the beginning stages of Alzheimer's. Now I see why Henry stayed on Cape Cod in his beautiful house with his beautiful wife and three beautiful children and their equally beautiful Labradoodle.

Manuel entered the kitchen, fortunately with his clothes on. "'Ello, Miss Sarah," he said, bowing his head. He clearly didn't know that I had seen him.

"So, Manuel? You are living on the property now?" I said, trying to hide the fact that I wanted to bite his nose off.

"Si. Mrs. O'Malley felt it be good idea para it is lonely for her." He walked over to the fridge and helped himself to a coke.

"So do you still do gardening work?" I asked.

"I do a little pruning."

"Yes . . . apparently to my mother!" I had raised my voice a little too loudly.

I was beginning to feel the effects of the vodka.

Manuel looked at me as if I had just shot him between the eyes. "I'm sorry . . . I don't understand!"

"Is everything okay down there?" my mother called from upstairs.

"It's fine mother," I answered, feeling embarrassed.

"I will go now, Señora." Sensing I was not happy, Manuel took himself out of the kitchen.

My mother appeared with her hair in a towel and what looked like an old bridesmaid's dress . . . no . . . wait . . . it was my high school prom dress!

"You look lovely, Ma . . . " I said, trying to mean it.

"Thank you, darling. I thought I would make you a sandwich now."

I suggested that I make dinner for the two of us if she felt like it, but she said she wasn't hungry and was going to go to bed early. I looked forward to going out for a quiet dinner alone with the book I was trying to finish.

It took almost forty-five minutes to get out of the house. My mother was determined to have me eat peanut butter. She kept saying, "But it's your favorite!"

That was certainly true forty-three years ago. My father used to tell the story of how when I was two years old he woke me up early to let my pregnant mother sleep. He led me into the kitchen and lifted me up onto the counter where I loved to sit and watch the goings-on. "Sarah, honey, what do you want for breakfast?" he asked.

"Peanut butter."

"No, honey, you can't have peanut butter. So what do you want for breakfast?"

I repeated, "Peanut butter."

"Sarah, you can't have peanut butter for breakfast. You can have peanut butter for lunch! Now what do you want for breakfast?"

"Lunch!" I replied.

As the story goes, I should've been a lawyer. Of course I got the peanut butter! My father always thought I was brilliant, until my sister Rachel came along. The funny thing was, I was never jealous of her. Even when our brother Henry was born everyone loved Rachel the most. Maybe it was some strange karmic thing. She would only be on this earth a short while, so however the planets aligned in the cosmos, it made sure that she was treated extra-specially for that time.

Henry and I had other assets and were certainly smart children. I just chose not to grow up to be what I probably should have been . . . a lawyer, doctor, thief.

Instead, I became a writer. My parents were not thrilled about that choice of career. What made things worse was that I wrote saucy, romantic novels. The ones with the Fabio look-alike on the cover. It was a surprise to me, too. I'd had very little passion in my life to draw on at that time. That's not to say there wasn't a lot of sex . . . There was certainly that! Just not a lot of wining and dining! That's probably why I wrote about it. As for Henry . . . he did become a doctor. A thoracic surgeon! Still, I always wondered what Rachel would have done with her life if we'd never set foot in that jewelry store.

"What do you think about this necklace, kids?" my father asked his three unruly children. Our father was trying to buy something nice for our mother for their anniversary. All we could do was chase one another around the store.

"Rachel, Sarah, and Henry, stop running around!!!" Our father demanded. He was a familiar face in town and being a college professor, he didn't want to be perceived badly. When he was angry, his voice became low and throaty.

Normally we would have stopped in our tracks if he spoke to us like that. For some reason the warning didn't work that day. Rachel was piggy in the middle. Henry and I had trapped her in the center of the store. As we both closed in on her from opposite sides, Rachel took off, laughing and screaming, trying to get away. I rewind the moment forever in my mind. I still don't really know how it happened. Just as Henry and I closed in, Rachel began to fall. It was all in slow motion. She flung her arms wildly trying to catch herself. I reached out for her, but I was too far away. Henry didn't move. The sound of breaking glass was the worst of it. It took years before that sound no longer haunted my sleep. She fell forward into the display case in front of her. The glass seemed to implode. There wasn't a lot of it on the ground. When our father picked her up, I didn't see any blood. Not at first. And then within seconds a trail of blood escaped from under her little arm.

"I'm okay, Daddy!" she said, looking up into his eyes.

And then the blood gushed like those spinning wheel paint kits; set a drop of paint on a wheel and it spins into a beautiful design. My dad cupped Rachel's armpit with his hand and started to run out of the store and down the street. Henry and I followed trying to keep up with him. The hospital was only a few blocks away so we just ran and ran.

Henry and I got to the hospital several minutes after our father. We followed the blood trail and tracked him through the emergency room doors. When we got inside, Rachel and Dad were nowhere to be seen. We asked the nurse behind the station if she knew where the man carrying the little girl went. The nurse's face registered alarm. She told us where we should wait and said she would get us some juice if we wanted. I had often wondered what it must've been like seeing a four-year-old and me, only eight, racing into the hospital alone. We sat and waited and waited for what seemed an eternity.

I couldn't believe how much blood covered my father when he finally came into the waiting room. He took one look at the two of us sitting there and a sound came out of him unlike anything I had ever heard before. He grabbed both of his remaining children and sobbed. Rachel was gone.

We didn't learn exactly what happened until days later. Glass had cut through a major artery under her armpit, and she bled to death. We didn't need the details in the hospital. In that moment our father's sobs were enough. There were no cell phones back then. No one could reach our mother. She had gone to the beauty parlor that day in anticipation of her anniversary dinner. My father was taking her to the Stone Manor Hotel and Restaurant, a fine Tuscan-style hotel in Marin County, a family favorite. Even as small children we had sophisticated pallets and very good manners.

When the three of us got home from the hospital and she wasn't back yet, we sat in the living room waiting for her. She looked radiant when she came through the door. Her hair glistened and had been slightly teased at the crown, giving her added lift. Normally my mother's hair was a mousy blonde, but that day it looked like spun gold. She was wearing a new white eyelet dress with tiny pearl buttons down the front. She must have gone to see her friend Sue, who worked in cosmetics at Saks, because her face was freshly made up. Standing in our hallway, she looked like an angel. It didn't take her long to evaluate the situation before her. With her smile still intact, she cautiously asked "What's wrong?"

My father stood up and began to walk over to her. I saw her eyes dart around the room like a wolf counting her pups . . . and then it sunk in . . .

"Where is Rachel?" . . . She asked in a low, slow voice, as if she already knew, and then collapsed into my father's outstretched arms.

"Oh God . . . Oh God!" she cried. Her body seemed to ache with pain as her sobs became louder and louder.

As I watched her I thought, "This is what it must look like when angels cry."

I don't remember anyone really speaking about what happened for a long time in our home. Henry and I always felt responsible for what had happened that day. And Rachel's death profoundly changed our parents' lives forever.

Driving into the driveway of Stone Manor Hotel, I realized I had avoided the place just as my parents had done since that fateful anniversary. It was difficult even to think about the place. We had celebrated birthdays here. We even had a Christmas Eve dinner here, and Santa stopped at the table. Rachel had asked him for a diary with a key. I wanted a doll that peed herself! Little did any of us know she would not live to see another Christmas. My parents not only never returned to the restaurant, but they never acknowledged their anniversary again.

I hadn't eaten anything all day. The thought of peanut butter had been tempting. But this restaurant served the best rib eye steak. My stomach growled, thinking about it. When I entered the handsome foyer, I felt strangely at home. Everything looked as it had for years. I veered off to the right toward the restaurant. As I walked through the lounge with the crackling fireplace, I heard someone say, "Is that little Sarah O'Malley?"

I turned to scan all the female, martini-drinking clones in the lounge and settled on Jocelyn Beckett. As usual, she was strikingly put together. At the age of seventy, she could pass for fifty. She looked better than I did! She walked toward me, her delicate ankles teetering on stilettos. I was thoroughly impressed. I hadn't worn heels in years!

"Hello, Jocelyn," I said as she approached.

"How's your dear mother?" She asked, shaking her head. Obviously, she had heard that my mother had lost her marbles.

"She's okay, thank you. You look great." I changed the subject.

"Divorce suits me!" She laughed.

I had heard about the Beckett divorce. My mother had described it as nasty.

"Obviously it suits you," I responded. "How's Marie?" Marie was Jocelyn's and Robert's first child. She and I had grown up together.

"She's terrific. Three kids. Great husband. Beautiful home!" I tried not to appear as jealous as I really was.

"And you remember my son, Terry? Well, he's running Robert's firm now," she said proudly.

Terry was eleven years younger than Marie. When we were teens, he would insist on driving us mad. In fact, when he was five years old, he walked in on Marie and me kissing. Both of us were virgins at fifteen and proud of it, but we wanted to have a little action. Rather than look to a pock-faced boy with dirty fingernails, we felt confident in each other's good hygiene. So we turned to one another for a little spice. To this day I think Marie was the best kisser I ever had.

Terry immediately ran to Jocelyn and told her we were kissing. Thank the Lord, she didn't believe him. Instead, she washed his mouth out with soap and made him say ten Hail Mary's in front of Marie and me.

Looking at Jocelyn, I could see that nothing had really changed about her. She still resembled a Stepford wife, only a little drunker.

"I'm excited to read the new book, Sarah," she winked. "I saw you on *The Today Show* last week!"

"Thank you Jocelyn. I'm excited to read it, too," I said, knowing how far behind I was with this one.

I excused myself and found the hostess, who sat me at a small table by the window. I promptly ordered a Pinot Noir and opened my Tumi laptop case. I checked my computer to see if I had any e-mails . . . nothing. Not even a word from either of my kids. I figured no one needed anything. I pulled up the pages of the new book I had just mentioned to Jocelyn. I was calling it: "***Tequila Sunrise Nights.***"

Maddie Keeler, a forty-year-old woman, takes a trip to Cabo San Lucas, after her husband leaves her for a twenty-year-old Cuban cabana boy. After sixteen years of marriage and two kids, she has her first vacation alone. Before too long, she meets Paul Rodriguez, the hotel manager, a beautiful six foot three Mexican with green eyes and a ten and a half inch appendage.

This book was taking way too long to write according to my agent. My publishers expected two books a year from me since my books had hit the best-seller list for a long time, they counted on me to deliver. And I was really late with book number two! And we were coming to the end of the year. Everyone knew that my life was falling apart. My husband had shacked up with his bimbo girlfriend. My seventeen-year-old daughter left to go to college. My recently divorced twenty-eight-year-old daughter had another miscarriage. And I just discovered that my mother needs to be committed to the looney bin! I'm amazed that I can string two words together at all!

None of that matters. They were still on me to "Get it done."

I began to read the last few lines I had written just a few days before . . .

With spasmodic ecstasy, her loins seemed to dance an internal meringue.

God this is awful!! I thought, reading it back to myself. After all, how many times can you describe hot sex? Especially if you aren't having any yourself?

His skilled tongue danced around her erect nipples making them so hard it was almost too much to bear. But she had never had a lover so unselfish, so concerned for her desires to be fulfilled. He slowly moved down toward her clean shaven mound, flicking his tongue ever so lightly . . . .

"Pardon me, would you like to see a menu?"

I jumped and looked up to see Mr. Abercrombie and Fitch standing before me. He looked as if he had stepped out of the pages of the catalogue and was lost. I responded in an extremely sophisticated manner. "Huh?" was all I could manage to get out.

"Would you care to look at a menu or do you know what you might want?" he asked.

"Oh yes, I know what I want," I said while thinking, "Do they serve you for dinner?" Did I say that out loud?

He smiled as though he knew exactly what I was thinking. I was never good at hiding my feelings.

"Rib eye, medium and fries, please." I said without making eye contact.

"Good choice." He smiled and took off.

I watched his butt as he walked away . . . probably gay, I figured. I stuck my nose back into my own business. It wasn't too long before I heard my name called again. Only this time by a deeper, sexy voice. I looked up to see another young, handsome man, this time a cross between J. Crew and Boy's with Harleys.

"It's me, Terry. Terry Beckett. Marie's brother . . . "

"Oh, my God," I said starting to rise.

"Please, don't get up." He put a hand on my shoulder. "I just heard you were here. I came to pick up my very intoxicated mother."

I smiled and asked him to sit down for a minute. He was charming, funny. Needless to say, my steak arrived as we were talking. There is no way to look ladylike when you're ravenous and have a huge chunk of meat in front of you. It didn't really matter. I mean, this was "Stinky Terry." The little boy who always had his finger up his nose.

He didn't stay long. He was worried that his mother would be face down in her baked Alaska by now. As he stood, I asked him to please give my love to Marie.

"Should I kiss her for you, too?" He smiled.

"You so don't remember that time."

"Which time are you referring to? I remember quite a few times over the years." He raised his eyebrows.

I felt my skin turning the color of my wine.

"Don't be embarrassed," he said. "I was just jealous that it was Marie and not me!" With that, he turned and left. I felt an unusual tingle between my legs. Something I hadn't felt in a long time. I was certain that I resembled that of the Cheshire Cat. A large grin was plastered across my face.

My G.Q. waiter asked if everything was okay. I told him I was fine.

"Did your boyfriend leave?" he asked.

"Boyfriend?" I snorted. "No . . . no, not a boyfriend. Well, yes a friend . . . an old friend. He's the brother of a close friend . . . " Why was I rambling? Thank God he didn't say your son!

"Good . . . so you're single?" he asked rather boldly.

"Ahh . . . yes," I stammered. This was really the first time I not only acknowledged being single, but realized that I actually was.

"Very good," he said, sauntering away.

"I have T-shirts older than you," I thought as that feeling between my legs got stronger.

I am considered an attractive woman, maybe even pretty, in some circles. I am finally comfortable with my five foot seven inch frame. I hated being tall in school. The boys were always so much shorter. What's up with that? But being tall suited me now. Only recently did I become a redhead again. I was a dull blonde, like my mother. After the divorce, I wanted to feel differently, and look differently.

He lived down the darkest, longest driveway. Even though the moon was full, I could barely tell where I was going. How did I get talked into giving him a ride home? Three glasses of wine and the complimentary dessert wine would be the answer to that question. I learned his name was Dwight. He mentioned he did some modeling here and there. He was thirty and looked twenty. And here I was with him in my car, in front of his house.

It's all a blur. His cock was in my mouth before I realized that it was. Within moments, I was standing in his kitchen and he hoisted me up onto the counter had my panties down, my skirt up, and his pants down, and he was thrusting the best tool I could remember having inside me. Mind you, it had been a while since anything other than a tampon had been there.

We went from room to room. From the kitchen, to the top of the washing machine, to the couch, then the recliner. I had forgotten what young male stamina was. Remember, I was at least fifteen years older than he, and my body wasn't in the kind of shape it had been, even a year ago! My nipples used to look toward the heavens. Now they look more like Marty Feldman's eyeballs. One stares off to the left and the other seems to be looking at my shoes. But Dwight kept telling me how beautiful and sexy I was, how he preferred older women and that I was hotter than anyone he had been with.

"Flattery will get you a blow job," I thought.

We finally ended up in his bed where he curled himself around me, like a newborn fawn, and fell into a deep sleep. It was simultaneously charming and alarming. When I slowly began to get up, he caught my arm.

"Don't go," he moaned.

"I have to . . . my mother will be worried! God, that sounded so highschool."

We both giggled. I leaned in for a small good night kiss, which ended up involving that tongue again and oh my . . . if he wasn't hard again.

I woke up the next morning in his bed.

My waiter!

Chapter Two

Inducted Into The Hall Of Blame

I crept as quietly as I could into the house. It was only six A.M. Roosters I know are still sleeping! But not Olivia Mancuso O'Malley. Nope . . . not my mother. I should've known. I remembered my first real date.

At sixteen, I was finally allowed to go alone to the movies with a boy. Jeremy Dion. He was eighteen, but we didn't tell my parents that. We went to the drive-in movies in his bright yellow, hatchback car. Naturally, we didn't tell them that either. He pulled his car into the parking space backwards, with the rear of the car facing the screen, so we could "watch" the movie lying down. Smooth, huh? He had a whole set up in the back of his car. He opened the hatchback and put down blankets and pillows. A huge bong had its own seat in the back, too. Even though Jeremy was a pock-faced boy, the sort that Marie and I warned each other about, he actually was very sweet and funny, and I was very horny. I knew what I was in for that night, and I was totally prepared. At least I thought I was.

When Jeremy started to kiss me, I became acutely aware that he was wearing Aqua Velva. I recognized the fragrance, because it was the same aftershave my grandfather wore. Apparently, Jeremy bathed in it. It was disconcerting, to say the least. As Jeremy plunged his tongue deeper into my mouth, all I could see before me was Grandpa Reginald. It didn't take long before Jeremy was exploring what was under my blouse. At sixteen, I was considered small busted. I was not as endowed as most of my friends. And I also had boy hips. What I wouldn't do to have that all now! At the time I felt unwomanly. Definitely not sexy.

Even now, I am still considered thin. My breasts are still too small for my frame, and my tiny waist disappeared after my second daughter, Lily was born. These days I spend way too much money trying to get rid of the gray hairs. Another reason I'm a red head at the moment. No middleman. I buy a box, smear on the goo and in minutes I'm good to go. Back then, though, I was definitely a blonde. Jeremy's favorite. And this night I was the blonde of choice.

We lit up his bong. I was sufficiently stoned after a few hits. I just hoped that I wouldn't start to laugh uncontrollably for no apparent reason. As soon as Jeremy was high, he mounted me as if I were a bitch in heat. Okay, at that point I was. We began rolling around. He on top of me. Me on top of him.

I could feel how hard he was through his button fly jeans. His erection caught me off guard. Until that point, I had never had a hard penis between my legs. When Marie and I fooled around, there was never penetration. A lot of rubbing and tongues but nothing like this! I could've cared less that his breath smelled like pizza, that he was panting and drooling like a bloodhound, and that he reeked of my grandpa. I just knew that he had to be inside me quick!

I began tugging at his pants, he with mine. The sounds he made convinced me that if I didn't get him soon, his tidy whities would be the recipient of what I wanted so badly. When he finally thrust himself inside me, I screamed. I was not prepared for the searing pain that I felt. Something about my scream got him even more riled up, and he came before I knew what had happened. To make matters worse, all I could hear in my head was "Is that all there is?" The song stayed in my head for about three days. I felt totally used and abused, but I realized that I had experienced some rite of passage. I was no longer a little girl. I felt that I could conquer the world. I was woman!

• • •

As I quietly let myself into my mother's house, after my night with Dwight, I relived that night with Jeremy. My mother was sitting in the same wingback chair with the same expression on her face. She had been up all night waiting for me. "Where were you all night?" she growled.

I thought about telling her to jump in the lake. I'm a middle aged, divorced woman . . . but that would be too mean. I just said "None of your business!"

She stood and glared at me. I excused myself, saying that I had to shower, and headed for the stairs.

She stopped me in my tracks about half way up. "Just wait till I tell your father you were out all night, young lady."

I turned to face her, and realized for the first time what was really happening to my mother. She looked so frail standing there. So hurt. It was as if I were sixteen again . . . for both of us.

"Oh, Mom . . . " was all I could say as I walked back down the stairs toward her. I wrapped her in my arms and felt her body let down. I think if I hadn't been holding her, she would have disintegrated. She began to cry softly at first and then she sobbed. Her body jerked and rocked in my arms.

As I held her firmly, tears welled up in my own eyes. This was only the second time I had seen my mother cry like this. The first time was after she had learned about Rachel. I wondered why she would be crying that way now.

"It was you . . . " she said ever so faintly, "you and Henry." She continued to sob.

"What about us, Mom?" I asked, still holding her up.

"She wouldn't be dead if it wasn't for the two of you!" She released herself from my grip and walked away.

I stood, frozen, stunned. After all these years, there it was. She blamed my brother and me for Rachel's death. It wasn't bad enough that he and I had blamed ourselves almost our entire lives. Now it was out in the open. However delusional she was, the picture was very clear.

It was my turn. I collapsed in a heap on the floor. I couldn't believe that I had that much bottled inside of me. I must have been on the hallway floor crying for half an hour. My entire body felt like putty. Now I knew where I stood in this family. How I was viewed by the one person I tried to please my whole life. There it was. I was a murderer.

• • •

It rained that day. It rained so hard the driver had the windshield wipers going full tilt. The sound reminded me of a heartbeat Da Thump, da thump, da thump, da thump. Our outfits matched. Henry wore overall shorts, and I was dressed in a jumper dress. They were black and had silver embossed fleur de lys on the bibs. I felt so grown up to be wearing black. We were never allowed to wear black. I was pleased with my brand new, black patent leather Mary Janes. I couldn't stop looking at them so shiny and new, with the smallest of heels. Yes, a heel.

I sat between my parents. My father kept putting his hand on my legs in a feeble attempt to stop me from swinging them. My mother sat staring out the car window. She wore large Jackie Kennedy glasses all the time. It didn't matter if we were home or at the market, she did not take them off for days. Henry sat across from us, in his own seat playing with his toy soldiers.

The limo slowed down, and we pulled into a driveway. I could see the sign that read 'funeral home'. A sea of umbrellas filled the parking lot. I couldn't see who had shown up, but I remember thinking it was the entire city. Grandpa Reginald, a fire captain, was my only living grandparent. He and some of his crew had arrived in their uniforms and fire trucks. Everything looked so official.

Our driver took us to the back of the building where a kind looking older woman waited for us in the doorway. The driver got out first and opened a gigantic umbrella.

"You guys go in first," my dad said to Henry and me.

"But dad, I . . . "

"Please Henry just do as I say!" There was that low stern voice again.

Henry and I climbed out of the car under the awaiting umbrella. Just as we were walking toward the older woman, I stepped directly into a puddle. A big, muddy, puddle. "My shoes!" I cried out. Henry started to laugh. "It's not funny, Henry," I yelled at him. The driver picked me up with his free arm while managing to keep all three of us dry, and he carried me to the open door. "There you go princess," he said as he lowered me down.

I looked at my new shoes. "They're ruined!" My white socks were splattered with mud and my shoes would never be the same.

"Come over here sweetheart," the older woman said. She put me in a chair and removed my shoes and socks. "Let me see what I can do," she said before disappearing into another room.

I didn't know why it was taking so long for my parents to come in. When Henry called my name from another room, I didn't consider waiting where I was. Bare-footed, I stepped onto fading carpet.

"Sarah, look at this," Henry called out. I followed his voice into the chapel. No one had been brought into this part of the building yet. The pews looked freshly polished. Candles burned next to an array of beautiful flowers. Henry was standing next to Rachel's open casket. It sent chills up my spine.

"Henry, get away from there!" I snapped at him.

"No, look, Sarah, she's sleeping!"

I couldn't help myself. It was like the pull of gravity. I couldn't resist looking, even though I really, really didn't want to. Since Henry was so young, his fascination with what he was seeing made sense. The casket was so tiny. It looked like a toy. The cherry wood was so highly polished you could see your reflection in the casket. As I approached, my heart raced, and for the first time in my eight years on earth, I began to sweat. I felt little beads forming just above my lip. I could hear the whooshing sound of my heart pumping in my ears. When I got to the coffin, I closed my eyes. I was so afraid to open them. Of course, I finally did.

I looked at Rachel, so beautiful, lying there. She did look as if she was sleeping. Her blonde ringlets were a golden halo around her tiny head. I touched her lips, which looked much redder than they were in real life. I thought "It might be make-up." I stood there waiting for her to open her eyes. I was convinced that she would.

The noise in my head got louder and louder, and the perspiration heavier. I started to feel nauseated. I became aware of the music in the chapel. "Amazing Grace" was being piped through the speakers. I heard Henry ask, "What's wrong?" Everything in the room began to spin around. Then it all went black. And so began a series of fainting episodes that continue to this day.

"Sarah? . . . Sarah . . . Dear God!" I heard my father's voice, swirling around in my head. When I finally opened my eyes, I was in an office, lying on a couch, my father bending over me with tears in his eyes. The kind lady who had helped with my shoes, put a damp cloth on my forehead. A huge clap of thunder outside caused me to bolt upright. I hated thunder. "You fainted, sweetheart," my father said.

"Where are my shoes?" was all I could reply.

The services had already begun without my father and me. When we walked into the chapel, the entire room went quiet.

I detected whispers . . . "She fainted" "Those poor children" "That's Sarah . . . the eldest."

The woman had cleaned up my shoes as best as she could but the socks were a lost cause. I had to wear my shoes without the socks which made them just a bit too big. As I walked, they slid off the back of my heels.

My mother did not look at me. I felt like an eight-year-old loser. I sat down next to Henry, aware that he felt it was his fault that I had fainted. At that moment, I understood he and I would feel responsible for so much in our lives.

The minister seemed to talk for days. I heard a lot of blowing noses and an occasional outburst of sobbing. I looked around and realized just how many people had come. Mrs. Robeck, the principal of our school, Tony and Jessie, the owners of the pizza parlor we frequented, Doctor Martin, the pediatrician. Even the paperboy sat in a pew next to his mother. I couldn't help wondering if they would have come for my funeral. At the end of the service, everyone got up and began to head out toward the parking lot. The cemetery was just above it on the hillside.

We stayed in the chapel so that we could say goodbye before they closed the lid of the coffin. My father went first. He looked inside Rachel's final resting place and just stared. He looked like a marble statue I had seen in a museum once. He didn't move. Then it was my mother's turn. She walked up, bent over, and kissed Rachel's forehead. I felt we should salute or something. She then told Henry and me to come over and kiss our sister good-bye. Henry went because he was told to. He was always a good little boy. I began to feel nauseated again. Bile came up in my throat.

Before I realized what I was doing, I took off running. I ran through the chapel, out the door, into the pouring rain, and began scaling the hillside behind the chapel. Tears flooded my face. Rain flooded my now too-big shoes, my ears, my mouth. I felt like I was suffocating. As I climbed higher and higher, I found myself imagining that I was getting closer to Rachel. I was doing what the minister said . . . I was "moving toward heaven."

I kept thinking "I'm coming, Rachel. I'll find you soon."

When I reached the top of the incline, all I saw were gravestones. I was now covered in mud. My heart ached so much I thought it would burst from my chest. I remember falling to my knees and saying over and over, "I'm sorry . . . I'm sorry."

Half the town had followed me up to this place. Concerned parents, teachers, neighbors, townspeople, saw me running and came after me. Though they were obviously concerned for my well-being, they terrified me. All the people who had run after me looked demonic. They, too, were covered in mud. Rain fell off their noses and foreheads. They were out of breath, as I was, from running up the steep, muddy hill. They panted and as they exhaled, the breath they expelled resembled ghosts. They called my name, but the howling wind made them sound like ghouls.

I don't remember exactly who reached me first. I think it was Tim, my father's assistant at the college. Whoever it was picked me up from the muddy ground where I had collapsed. He carried me up a winding path to what would be my sister's ultimate resting place.

The hearse and my parents weren't far behind. The tiny coffin that held my sister was carried by some of my parent's friends. There were so many umbrellas.

The minister said some final words and what used to be Rachel was lowered into the ground. My father made a noise that I hope never to experience again in my life. Like a coyote bringing home his kill, he lifted his head and began to howl. He wailed into the storm as the dirt and mud were pushed on top of my sister's beautiful casket.

I realize now that it is normal to have a gathering after someone dies. At the time, I thought it strange that everyone was eating and drinking and some people were laughing about things that had nothing to do with what had just taken place. My mother was AWOL from the beautifully catered event at our house. She was upstairs and we were told she was not to be disturbed.

My brother and I sat in the TV room and watched cartoons. My father made the rounds, thanking everyone for coming. Once everyone had left, my mother materialized and headed straight for the vodka. My father told us we should go to bed, but my mother nixed the idea. She wanted us to sit and listen to her talk about how beautiful and radiant Rachel had been. We sat watching mother get more and more drunk as our father tried, unsuccessfully, to defuse the potentially explosive situation.

Mother asked us to wait and disappeared into the other room. She returned, carrying the outfits we'd just worn for the funeral. In an impromptu ritual, she babbled words from the Bible and tossed our clothes into the fireplace. All of us sat staring at the burning clothing. My father used a poker to prevent embers from escaping. We sat until the last piece of anything recognizable had been incinerated. "Okay, you two, off to bed," my mother said as if nothing had just happened. And for the next few months, she behaved as if nothing had happened.

• • •

I discovered that the ability to forget was still with her. Though no longer sobbing, I remained in a heap on the floor. My mother came back into the hallway as she had done so many times before and behaved as if nothing had happened between us a few minutes prior.

"Sarah? What are you doing on the floor? You'll get dirty," she scolded.

"Oh, nothing, Mother," I responded from the floor. "I just realized what you've thought of me the last thirty or so years and thought I'd have a good cry!" Of course, I didn't actually say that. I just told her that I had lost a contact lens, assuming she probably wouldn't remember that I don't wear contact lenses.

"Well then, why not go get yourself ready for a nice lunch," she suggested in a cheerful tone. She disappeared into the kitchen and out the back door to visit Manuel. I heard giggling in the garden a short time later. The last thing I wanted to do was investigate as I wouldn't be able to handle the shock of anymore geriatric romping.

Since I had barely slept the night before, I decided to try and get some rest. I would figure out what to do with my mother and myself for the rest of the day later.

I could smell his cologne before I actually saw him.

I must have been sleeping so soundly. I had no idea how he got into my room. But there he was, standing over me with a colossal hard on inside his pants. I couldn't speak . . . nor did I want to at that moment. Instead of asking all the obvious questions like "How the hell did you get in here?" I did what any cock loving woman would do. I pulled down his pants and began licking and sucking his dick. He moaned as I pulled down the bed sheet, exposing the tiny tank top and thong I was wearing. My nipples were so hard he couldn't resist pinching them. His hand slipped into my panties where he found my wet pussy. He backed away from my mouth and ripped my panties off. His face was between my legs before I could catch my breath. His tongue was soft and hot. He knew every crevice that needed to be discovered. I used to beg my husband to try to think in Hebrew. To write backwards with his tongue . . . spell something! Anything! He was clueless. But Roberto—Latin lover that he was—knew how to make a woman shudder with ecstasy.

I closed my laptop. I was sure that if I e-mailed what I had been working on to my agent, she'd stop pressuring me for a little while. I never did get the nap in. It was beginning to get dark, and we hadn't even had lunch yet. I decided to go downstairs to see if Mother had returned from the alien ship. My stomach growled as I went to the fridge for a snack. I couldn't believe the eclectic array inside my mother's Sub Zero. Everything from jalapeños to Swiss chocolate to bologna. My mother hates bologna. Clearly I was going to have to do some shopping soon. I pulled out the jar of martini olives, which I opened as I sat at the kitchen table, and popped one into my mouth. I loved the salty tang of martini olives. My father always allowed me to take one from his martini glass when I was little. They had the slightest taste of vodka that made me feel grown up eating them. He taught us kids how to mix drinks by the time we were around five years old. We were little party tricks for guests. Sometimes I would take the olives and put them on my fingers, then pretend I was doing magic, as I slipped them into my mouth, making them disappear. I would get a rounding applause from our inebriated guests, and I felt special.

"Sarah Jean? Mr. Hollis would like a scotch and soda with a twist of lime, please." My father would chuckle as he watched me carefully pour a jigger of scotch and top it off with the soda. We weren't allowed to use a knife to cut the lemons or limes. Our mother would make sure they were prepared beforehand. We were like a Lilliputian lounge act. When our parents socialized and became more intoxicated, I would play with the olives and my brother would steal the booze. During one dinner party, I found Henry passed out in the middle of the stairway. He had found the cherry brandy and consumed most of it. He was six at the time.

I heard my mother's voice from outside. Pulling back the café curtain, I saw my mother and Manuel in the garden. Olivia's garden. She was tending to it as Manuel looked on. She was bent down just inside the white arbor that was heavy with climbing roses. We used to call this "The Secret Garden," because mother would often disappear into it for hours. She had an extensive array of herbs that she used in her cooking. Her hydrangeas were in full bloom, the flowers a stunning sky blue. The snapdragons stood proudly erect. I found myself smiling, realizing that this was one part of mother's life that remained the same.

There was a knock at the door. My mother either didn't hear it or chose to ignore it as she kept busy with the roses. I went to the front door barefooted. When I was a little girl, I always loved to answer the front door and would race my siblings to see who could get there first. I imagined finding someone on the other side with a fabulous present. Something that was just for me! A puppy? A fancy dress? A pony! My little body would pull and yank at the heavy door, hoping to find something special on the other side. As middle-aged me opened the door, I was surprised to see Terry Beckett, Marie's little brother, standing under the eave on the front porch.

"Sarah, it's good to see you again so soon," he said with a big smile. He was carrying a briefcase and was wearing a tailored suit and tie.

"God, please don't tell me you've become a Jehova's witness!" I blurted out.

"God, no," he laughed. He looked adorable, especially with a five o' clock shadow. I must have been staring because he asked if he could come in as if I maybe wasn't going to allow him inside.

"Of course. Please. I'm sorry," I stammered. He brushed passed me, his body lightly rubbing against mine. Tiny hairs stood at the back of my neck. I was surprised at how handsome he had become. I guess I hadn't really noticed the night before, but I could see that his eyes were the deepest brown, his jaw line wide, and distinguished looking. He asked if my mother was home, and I told him that she was gardening.

"Is there anything I could help you with?" I asked. I guided him into the living room where I motioned him to sit on the checked couch. He opened his briefcase and brought out a large file.

"I'm not sure if your mother has told you anything or how much I can reveal to you."

"Well, I suppose I won't be able to answer that until I know what you are talking about."

"Are you aware that your mother owes quite a bit of money on this house?"

This was totally puzzling. I explained that my parents had been in this house for forty-five years. I assumed that they had owned it outright for years.

"Look, maybe I should talk to Olivia"

"When is the last time you spoke to my mother?"

"About a month ago," he replied.

"So you are aware that she is suffering from dementia? That's why I'm here at the moment, to try to help her with things . . . "

Terry dropped his eyes.

"How much money we talkin' about?" I braced myself.

"A hundred thousand dollars."

"What?" I screamed. "How the holy hell is that possible?"

Sitting back in his seat Terry assumed the position a therapist would take. I had experienced being on the couch during analysis in my younger days. The way he stretched himself out before me he looked like the patient. Terry's mouth was indeed moving but I was unable to hear anything he was saying. Beads of sweat formed themselves above my top lip and forehead. I only caught the essence of some of his sentences. Music began in my head and I began recalling a particular chapter in "*The Therapy Couch*" I had written a few years back.

Entry: September 20 1892. Patient Elizabeth Von R.

Day 12 of Elizabeth's treatment.

It had occurred to me after her sister's initial visit regarding Elizabeth, that her condition may be psychosomatic. That she had consciously put herself into the wheelchair. She described her last dream:

"I was in a ballroom. It was illuminated only by candlelight. I was very out of breath. But I stood alone on the giant dance floor.

Helmut entered and we stood looking at one another for a long time. He had been riding and carried a large riding crop. His free arm wrapped around my waist and we begin to move. Swaying to unheard music. Our dance becomes more intimate and we begin to move faster. More in unison. He begins to flick me lightly with his riding crop. And I feel excited. I begin to moan and he hits me harder the next few times. I can feel him becoming hard inside his trousers. We twirl and twirl. I am becoming dizzy. Dizzy from the movement and dizzy from what I feel deep inside. Then I hear a woman's voice call "Helmut." I look, and it is my sister Marta. Helmut, her husband, breaks his grip from me but I cannot stop twirling. I spin and spin until I fall to the ground. I cannot move, and I am alone now. My wheelchair is on the other side of the room."

It has been apparent to me that the feelings Elizabeth harbors for her brother-in-law are very deep. Although at twenty-three she is still a virgin and believes she is incapable of being married or having a fulfilling sexual relationship. I shall be experimenting with Freud's theory of psychosexual development in an attempt to prove her wrong. I shall try hypnosis first.

Elizabeth's Diary

I shall be seeing Doctor Van Damm again tomorrow. He believes he can help me and that I indeed can feel below my waist. I laughed in his face my last session. It isn't as though I threw myself down those stairs three years ago. I slipped. He believes it was a deliberate accident because it was Marta's wedding day and I wanted to ruin it for her. What a horrible, silly thing to believe. But if the doctor thinks I may be able to walk again I shall do whatever it takes to do so!!

The next morning it was raining. Elizabeth was being wheeled into Doctor Van Damm's house by her sister Marta. The doctor's assistant, Nurse Sutter, said that she would take Elizabeth and

Marta should wait in the lounge. Nurse Sutter was a young and beautiful woman. Elizabeth had seen her before. She worked in the doctors "examination" room and Elizabeth had never been in that room before. She had always been in the doctor's office on his couch during her analysis.

As the nurse opened the door to the new room, Elizabeth was caught off guard by how cold and sterile this room was. There was a large examination table in the middle of the room and a variety of medical devices and electrical apparatus. She hadn't a clue what they could be used for. Elizabeth felt herself becoming nervous now. Sensing this, the nurse reassured her that all would be fine and that she would stay in the room with her.

Nurse Sutter helped Elizabeth onto the examination table and explained that she had to disrobe.

"I have to be naked?" Elizabeth asked nervously.

"Yes, Elizabeth, you do!" The nurse said as she began to unbutton Elizabeth's blouse first, revealing the top of her slip. She motioned for Elizabeth to lie down and then began to unfasten the tiny hooks at the side of her skirt. Nurse Sutter folded everything neatly as she continued to take off more clothing.

"It is cold in here," Elizabeth, now only in her slip and stockings, complained.

"It won't be for too long now," the nurse assured her, removing her slip.

Doctor van Damm entered the room in a white coat. He wore a suit and tie during therapy sessions. It was rather alarming for Elizabeth to see him this way.

"Good morning Elizabeth. Are you ready?" The doctor asked as he held her hand.

"I believe so."

"Then let us begin."

Nurse Sutter turned out the main light, leaving on only the soft light above the table.

"I want you to close your eyes now," the doctor directed. "Imagine with each breath you are descending down a flight of stairs. With each breath you get deeper, and you will trust everything that I am saying and doing. Yes?"

Elizabeth nodded. Within a few minutes, Elizabeth was in a deep trance.

"I want to take you back, Elizabeth, to a time when you were a young girl. A teenager. The time your mother found you in the lake . . ."

Elizabeth began to moan.

"I went to the water. It was such a warm day."

Doctor Van Damm and Nurse Sutton begin to touch Elizabeth's head and neck slowly, with just their fingertips.

"Go on," said the Doctor.

"I took all my clothes off as there was nobody around. The water was cool."

"How did it feel on your body?" The doctor asked as his fingertips began to move down her body.

"I felt aroused."

"Did you touch yourself?"

Elizabeth nodded.

Nurse Sutton opened a drawer that contained many different pieces of equipment. She pulled out a metal phallic shaped tool and plugged it into an outlet. She handed the primitive dildo to the doctor. He took the tool and placed it just above Elizabeth's vagina. It vibrated slowly.

"Were you able to take yourself to orgasm?"

Elizabeth shook her head, no.

"My mother found me. She saw what I was doing and became very angry. She pulled me out of the water by my hair."

"Then what did she do to you, Elizabeth?"

The doctor motioned to the nurse to grab something from the corner of the room. He put the vibrator now directly on Elizabeth's vagina as the nurse walked back toward the doctor with a bamboo switch.

"My mother grabbed a long branch . . . " Elizabeth paused.

"She hit you with it, correct?"

She nodded.

"Like this?" The doctor said, indicating to Nurse Sutton to begin to hit Elizabeth on her legs with the switch.

"Yes!" Elizabeth moaned. "She kept hitting me."

Elizabeth's body began to sway and rock on the table as the doctor held the vibrator on her vagina. The nurse continued to lightly flog her legs, her stomach, her breasts.

"What happened as she was hitting you Elizabeth?"

She can't take it any longer. Elizabeth cried out. "Oh God! Oh God!"

Her body violently jerked and shook. Her toes began to curl and her legs quaked as she was brought to an extreme climax.

Entry December 14 1892

Patient Elizabeth Von R

After the first of several psychosexual experiments my patient no longer used her wheelchair. We had broken through a deep rooted barrier that involved being in love with her brother-in-law and finding that she could only be satisfied sexually by being mis-treated. Her guilt drove her to cause herself to have a violent acci-dent, to avoid facing those demons.

Elizabeth's Diary

I had another dream. Only I was awake. Helmut came to me in the night while Marta slept. I was sitting at my mirror, combing my hair. I saw his reflection in the mirror. He stood with just his undergarments on. I was in my nightgown. I stood, in front of him, which I hadn't been able to do in years. He took down the straps of my nightgown which quickly fell to the floor, leaving me naked in front of him. He pulled me into his arms and we began to dance. We twirled until we found my bed. He kissed me passionately on the lips. I turned over presenting my virginal backside and he thrust himself immediately into my vagina as I screamed . . .

I was on the floor. I remembered Terry saying something about my father and a loan. Then the theme from Saturday Night Fever came into my head, and I was down for the count.

"Sarah!!?? You with me?"

I was staring up at the ceiling. "I am on the floor!"

"I think you fainted. Never seen anything like it. You started singing . . . something?"

"Bee Gees!"

"Yeah! And then your eyes rolled back into your head and . . . "

"Just help me up, please." This was enough humiliation for one day—second time I found myself in a heap on the floor.

He propped me up against the couch and went to get me some water.

"Get outta here!!" Mother screamed from the kitchen. "Get out! Rape! Fire! Hellllppp!"

Terry ran back into the living room with my mother on his heels wielding a hydrangea stalk like a samurai sword. Manuel quietly appeared behind my mother embracing her in a gentle but firm bear hug.

"Olivia, we must put your flower in *agua* before it dies," he whispered in her ear.

I learned a lot in that moment about the two of them. My mother completely transformed in an instant, from a killer banshee to Doris Day. She turned her head towards him. "You are right, Manuel. It needs a beautiful vase." Ignoring me on the floor she headed back toward the kitchen then stopped and looked back at Terry. "Oh, hi Terry . . . my you've grown so."

While she was leaving the room, she told Manuel that she'd known Terry since the day he was born and that his sister and I were such good friends.

"I know, *mija,* I know," I heard Manuel respond.

Terry leaned in and gave me a hand, finally, peeling me off the floor.

"See what I mean?" I asked.

He nodded, aware of my mother's condition. He said we should talk at another time. He would discuss the situation further with his father and partners.

I led him to the door. He turned and asked if I'd like to have dinner. "We could catch up on the last twenty years of being strangers, and I could fill you in a little bit more regarding your mother."

It was funny that looking at big/little Terry made butterflies swirl in my stomach. "Sure," I said, hoping to sound nonchalant.

"Great . . . see you at seven." He spun on his heels and went down the front steps.

"Wait," I called out. "Tonight? You mean tonight?"

He shrugged his shoulders and yelled back "Why wait?" He was in his sports car and down the driveway in a jiffy, leaving me wondering what was up with these younger men.

Later that evening, in a dismal attempt at being cool, I slipped on my way too-high heels and sauntered into the Stone Manor Hotel again. Hadn't been there in years and I was back two nights in a row. Wouldn't you know it Terry was sitting at a table with my waiter serving him. The heel of my foot slipped out of my six-inch fuck-me pumps just as I entered the dining room. Everyone, including the moose head on the wall saw me stumble. I looked back over my shoulder at the imaginary person, who had obviously pushed me and held my head high as if nothing had happened.

"Sarah!" They said in unison as I approached. Then looked at each other uncomfortably.

I tried to sit down before the gentlemen could fight over who would pull the chair out for me, but to no avail. Terry stood, just as my waiter reached for my chair and pulled it out for me. I made a strange gurgling noise in my throat, because words didn't seem to want to come out. I tried to will my skin from turning too pink and blotchy.

"Glad you could make it," Terry said, sitting back down.

"Nice to see you again, Sarah," my waiter said as he placed my napkin firmly between my legs. I watched him walk away in his crisp white jeans knowing that he was sans underwear.

Dinner was a constant battle of wills. I was trying to give Terry my undivided attention but was unable to stop looking at Dwight. I felt as if I had multiple personalities with an additional co-dependent personality thrown in, who was all about making sure neither guy knew what was really happening. Terry was being extremely attentive, but I couldn't help thinking about what I knew was in Dwight's jeans. It didn't help that the outline of his substantial cock was visible. What was wrong with me?

I tried talking business. After all, that's what brought me to this dinner in the first place. Alright, maybe the chemistry I felt earlier had a little to do with it. More than that, I had to find out what had happened to the house and what it meant for my mother. Sitting opposite Terry, I was so conscious of the little boy who would sneak into his sister's room because he heard noises.

Chapter Three

The Accidental Lesbian

Marie's little brother would often creep from his bed to spy on the two of us. Our friendship started off innocently enough. When we were twelve, Marie and I were inseparable. We told each other everything—every crush, every dream, every goal. Around this time we discovered what our bodies were about.

We would often lie in Marie's twin bed together and play the game "guess the body part." With our eyes closed, one of us would take the other's index finger and guide it to one of our body parts. Usually it was an eyeball, an inner ear, a tooth, or the inside of a belly button. We would laugh and squirm and feel as if we were doing something taboo. The older we became, the more forbidden the game grew.

One night, Marie took my hand, as usual, and placed it in a warm, wet place. Marie had a death grip on my hand. She held it in between her legs as she began to move her hips, ever so slightly at first. Within seconds, her breathing became faster, and she started to moan. I couldn't figure out what she was doing, because I wasn't doing a damn thing. My hand was perfectly still, but her body was rising and thrashing about. Suddenly her body jerked, and she let out a high-pitched groan. Then she lay motionless. After about a minute, I began to wonder whether I had just killed my best friend. She hadn't moved or spoken. I sat up to see if she was breathing. Her parents always kept the pool illuminated, which cast an eerie glow into Marie's dark bedroom. I looked at her face. She looked serene.

"Marie? Are you okay?" I whispered.

The beginnings of a smile slowly crept across her face. "*Le petit mort*," she said, her voice low.

"What??" I asked.

"*Le petit mort*," she repeated.

"Little death?" I had no idea what she was getting at. "Marie, what are you talking about?"

"What just happened to me. It's what they call it in France!" She giggled.

I threw myself back on the bed totally missing the joke. I didn't think she and I had any secrets from one another. Why now? And what was it that had to be said in French for crying out loud? I knew she had been reading Anais Nin, but I didn't know anything about what the books contained. Feeling extremely left out, I began to cry uncontrollably. Huge body-wracking sobs. Like a baby.

Marie sat bolt upright and stared down at me. "Oh my God, Sarah, what's wrong? What happened?"

I couldn't answer her as I really didn't know myself.

Marie did what any loving best friend would do. She wrapped me in her arms, cradling and rocking me gently back and forth, smoothing out the stray hairs that were now stuck to my forehead. Feeling so safe in her arms, I eventually stopped crying. Before too long, the two of us drifted into a blissful sleep.

I woke up the next morning with a strange sensation. Marie was balanced on one elbow. She had found my most vulnerable place between my legs with her free hand. She confidently smiled as she rubbed me over my pajama bottoms. Neither one of us spoke. I was alarmed by what was happening, but I wasn't brave enough to tell her to stop. The sensations I began to feel were totally new to me. I had heard of people masturbating. I knew that my brother had jerking off contests with his friends. I heard them discussing it one night. I was disgusted by the thought. I wasn't sure if the hole in my stomach I was experiencing was a result of being weirded out or was I enjoying what was happening? If I thought about it, I might have bolted out of the room, never to return again, but my body, paralyzed by fear and longing, kept me from moving. My hips slowly began rocking to a new beat. I closed my eyes and began to ride on this unexpected journey. I could hear my heart beating in my head. I wondered if I would pass out as I had done so often? At least I was in a prone position this time. Our breath was now in syncopation. I heard myself moan out loud. Taking the cue, Marie's hand disappeared into my pajamas and found my buried treasure. Even I had never touched myself down there, in that way at least. How did my best friend know how to do these things?

"Just let go, Sarah," I heard Marie's voice whisper, her breath hot on my neck now.

"I don't know . . . "

Marie leaned over and placed her lips on mine. Her tongue plunged deeply into my mouth. The rhythm of her tongue matched the rhythm of her fingertips. Without any sort of warning my body seemed to explode. My toes curled, my back arched into a rigid contortion. A shriek echoed in the tiny, morning lit room.

"Oh my God!" It took several seconds before I realized that it had been my voice. After my body released a final shudder and I found that I was still alive, the oddest thing happened. I began to cry as I had the night before. And then, like a crazy person, I began to laugh. I was crying and laughing, which of course made Marie start to laugh. The two of us must have laughed and cried for an hour. We never spoke about what we began to do with each other during our fifteenth year. Not even to each other. It was our dirty little secret.

Our trysts defined my early sexual life. After the loss of my "virginity" in the back of Jeremy's car, I had only one other sexual experience with a penis. It involved my high school biology teacher. I was seventeen and he was twenty-five . . . and a half, and was absolutely gorgeous. It all began when I stayed a little late after school to draw diagrams of various fungi. I happened to be a very good artist. It wasn't long before I was dropping off my fungus sketches at Mr. Runnels's apartment. We would sit and look at his books on anatomy and talk about the sexual differences between men and women. Within a few months, we began a series of our own experiments involving the human anatomy.

I learned how to be a proficient felator. He told me to treat his appendage as if I were having a yogurt push up. "Don't let it melt . . . " he would preach as I licked and sucked. Even though he had a wonderful looking penis—ok I had only seen one before—when he thrust himself deep within the core of my womanhood, I was never able to have an orgasm. It drove him nuts, which was actually a lot of fun for me. I became a puzzle to him. A challenge. A mystery he had to solve. So we tried everything. Backwards, forwards, doggie style, missionary, sixty-nine, and handcuffs. I have to say I had a great time. It wasn't as if I wasn't satisfied. It all felt amazing. I just couldn't cum. That only happened when I was with Marie. Go figure. Maybe it just all boiled down to trust.

Once in college, I found it was totally acceptable for girls to find themselves in other girls' beds. I felt I belonged there, too. It wasn't as if I felt like a lesbian or anything. I was actually more than attracted to men. Tall men, short men, men with really long hair and jeans, or short-haired preppy guys in suits . . . it didn't matter, I found them quite desirable. I just didn't have sex with them. I was petrified that I would feel like a failure if I could not achieve an orgasm with someone of the opposite sex. Being with a woman was obviously very narcissistic. It was like looking in a mirror. I knew all the mechanics of how the machine worked. After all, I had the same machine. By the time

I was in college, I had learned that I wouldn't go to hell, and my eyesight would remain intact if I touched myself. I had become quite proficient in the art of masturbation, so, when I touched a woman, it was like touching myself. Loving myself. Something I had trouble with.

I became a proficient liar as well when I met my future husband, because I was sleeping with my English teacher, Danielle. Brad was a law student, two years ahead of me. We met at a party given by a mutual friend. I almost didn't go, because I had a date with Danielle that night. She cancelled due to a severe head cold. Understanding that the last place she would want her stuffy nose was between my legs, I opted to be a brave girl and party. I dressed up in my favorite bohemian skirt and a paisley off-the-shoulder top. I laced up my moccasin boots and wore all things patchouli. Every part of me smelled of it. Patchouli oil was without a doubt the best invention for hiding the smell of marijuana. Before long, parents and local authorities figured that one out. But I truly loved the smell of it. The musty, earthy, sexiness of it.

Stephanie's apartment also smelled of patchouli. Good sign, I thought. The lights were low, and candles burned inside various wine bottles. A lava lamp bubbled in one corner, and a giant bong had center stage in the middle of the living room floor. I knew a couple of the people worshipping the bong God, but as I looked around, I realized I barely knew a soul.

Brad was on a couch in the corner of the room. He was hard to miss. His jet-black curls framed his round baby face. His eyes were whitish blue, and his eyelashes were three layers deep. I instinctively took my hair off its resting place on top of my head and let it fall in its wave of curls down to my waist. My hair was definitely one of my best features. I felt more than womanly when it was down. It worked, as I knew it would. I got Brad's attention. I felt the blood rush to my face, and I feared I looked like a cat in heat. He flashed a huge grin my way.

We spent several hours in our own little bubble. People occasionally spoke to us, but the only voices we seemed to hear were our own.

He was smart and funny and he told me he wanted to be a lawyer. I would learn in the latter stages of our marriage how talented a lawyer he was. I could never win an argument no matter how absolutely right I was. Even if I had proof of something, Brad could turn the whole thing around somehow and convince me that I had been wrong or had misinterpreted the facts. Inevitably I would feel guilty and not know why. The very decent living he made as a lawman only confirmed my suspicions that he was brilliant.

That first night, Brad made me laugh till my sides hurt. When he asked me back to his apartment, I went. We walked about two blocks from the school with our arms hooked together. We turned down a tree-lined street that was known as the better part of town and slipped into a quaint two story building. His apartment was not at all typical of a twenty-one-year-old student. It was immaculate with very beautiful furniture for a fellow student to have. I was used to bean bags and pillows on the floor. This guy actually had a dining table with chairs which I later learned had been imported from France. He offered me a drink from his well-stocked bar.

"Scotch?" he asked.

"Sure, why not?" I hated scotch, but I was liking the guy.

Once we made it to the bedroom, it was a tornado of clothing. Things flew around the room and ended up behind things, under things, hanging from things. We had a very difficult time finding a sock the next day.

Then and there, sitting on top of that man's cock, I had the orgasm of a lifetime. Maybe that was all my problem was . . . I needed to be on top for more than a few seconds. Years later, we girls would hear about the "G" spot. Obviously, I had found it! Gee!

I became a research scientist and a juggler at the same time. I had to juggle Danielle and Brad, but even more importantly, I had to make sure that my newfound orgasmic ability wasn't a fluke. I decided I should try to fuck as many guys as I could to make up for lost time. My ultimate goals were to stop falling in love with Brad and to put an end to my love affair with my teacher. I did want to have babies one day. Our age difference was a factor. I was eighteen, and she was thirty-five, a definite strike against us. She was so deep in the closet, our relationship had no future.

I went about fucking and sucking my way through junior year, all the while excusing my behavior as an experiment. I had to find out the truth about the big O. The holy grail. Okay, just my hole-e-grail. I could justify my behavior. I wasn't the only person conducting these sorts of experiments. It was college, after all! As long as the sex was safe we felt we could justify our behavior. Bottom line was I wanted to know exactly how my body worked and how I could be sufficiently satisfied. What's wrong with that? The question became, did I need to be filled with a penis? Or could I live with the occasional tongue or hand job on my privates without penetration? It was becoming clearer to me that I could not. Danielle began to notice I wasn't spending as much time with her. She realized I must be seeing someone else. I'm sure it didn't occur to her that I was seeing the entire local Air Force base.

Sex with Danielle had become calculated and aggressive, on my part anyway. My sexual escapades resembled being thrown around a room like a football waiting for the proverbial "touchdown" at the end. And sex with women didn't offer that. I slowly pulled back and felt badly about it. She had been a huge influence on me. I discovered that all the things I loved about her, at the beginning, the way her hair smelled of Herbal Essence shampoo, the way she didn't wear make-up, the way she breathed while she slept, started to bother me. I wanted her to remain my mirror. Instead the person looking back at me now was me.

I began seeing Brad more often. Since I thought about him all the time, it made sense. He made me laugh when we talked and cry when we made love. No one else had been able to do that. So I fell in love. I also recorded data from my "experiments." I documented so much of my life, then unaware that within three years out of college, I would publish my first novel titled *Love and Lust at Midnight*.

Eighteen-year-old Gwendolyn, a beautiful equestrian, has a summer fling with a twenty-five-year-old polo player, who likes to fuck standing up with his riding boots on.

The sun caused tiny beads of sweat to form across his collarbone. All I wanted to do was taste the saltiness of it on my tongue. Being the good girl everyone thought I was, I concentrated on cleaning the horse's hooves. The pick in my hand dug out the dirt that had accumulated that day from rain-drenched Charleston soil. I had difficulty concentrating as I couldn't help looking at Christopher's shoulders flexing as he brushed the bay mare's coat.

"How's it coming, Bridgit?" he called over to me.

"It's fine except the mud is really caked in this hoof," I answered.

"Here, let me take a look." Christopher gently took the horse's hoof and set it on top of his own thigh. He touched my hand and took the pick from it. I felt an electric charge between us. "See, it's not that hard," he said, looking up at me while peeling the mud from the horseshoe.

"No, I guess it isn't," I agreed.

Chris stood, in his white polo pants and boots, shirtless and sweating. He took my seventeen-year-old hand and placed it firmly on his crotch.

"But this is hard," he said, grinning.

I could feel the strength and the hardness of his manliness ready to burst free from the constraints of those riding pants.

Without another word, I slowly unzipped him and allowed his cock to spring free. He hoisted me up onto his hips and bent me down onto the haystack. He threw back my skirt and ripped my panties off in one sweeping motion. Placing himself above me, he positioned the tip of his cock at my awaiting, hungry orifice.

"This is my first time," I said, looking in his steely blue eyes.

"I'll be gentle," he said slowly gliding himself into my womanhood.

Marie got married, in the fall, just a year after graduating. Of course, I was her maid of honor. It was mind-blowing to me that my best friend would even consider marriage. David, her groom, was a billionaire's son, and he wasn't half bad looking. I guess I couldn't blame her.

The night before the wedding, it became apparent to the two of us that we would be locked forever in a secret world that only she and I knew about. To everyone on the outside looking in, there was nothing abnormal about two best friends spending the night together in the bride's hotel room. They would never know that we slept in the same bed, made love as if there was no tomorrow, and wept in each other's arms afterward. Little did I know that not only would this "big day" be life altering for Marie, but that my life would also change in an instant.

The morning of the wedding I awoke in the crook of Marie's arm with a horrible, nagging nausea in the pit of my stomach. I was sure it was all in my head. I mean I was really emotional. I launched myself toward the toilet bowl and began retching. Marie stood in the doorway and asked, "Are you pregnant?"

My whole world spun out of control.

Chapter Four

Fasten Your Seat Belts. It's Gonna Be A Bumpy Ride

"Are you alright?" Terry had been discussing my mother and the house. How we could possibly keep the house, how we should consider selling the house, how I should maybe put my mother in assisted living.

I noticed that my spaghetti had been in a continual twirl, never reaching my mouth. I probably could knit mittens by the time this meal ended. It was just so difficult to take him seriously. Here was little Terry, Marie's ten-years-younger brother looking like a ripe peach waiting for me to take a bite. I had to remind myself that he was just too young and that it would more than complicate things. He was only a few years older than my waiter. It felt wrong to be thinking these nasty things. Terry finished the rest of his meal. I didn't eat a thing but managed to sip my wine.

Dwight sashayed over with the check.

"You know, maybe you should meet with my father as well," Terry suggested. "Even though he's semi-retired. Since he is familiar with this issue I'm sure, he could help you come up with a solution."

We had a momentary struggle over the bill. I grabbed it first, but Terry insisted on paying. I wasn't going to argue.

Dwight returned to the table. As he picked up the bill, he also helped me out of my chair. With his hand on the small of my back, a little lower than what would be a casual motion, he said how great it was to see me again so soon and that he hoped to see me more often. An involuntary giggle escaped my throat, and I saw Terry's eyes flash with the knowledge that something intimate had passed between this waiter and me. In true pissing contest fashion, Terry replaced Dwight's hand with his own and guided me gently out into the parking lot. For the first time in a long time, I was beginning to feel beautiful. Maybe mid-forties isn't the end of the world!

I really hadn't anticipated an awkward moment before we said good-bye. Having known Terry his whole life, I felt that a good, warm bear hug would be appropriate. As I moved in, arms outstretched, he placed his hand behind my neck and pulled me to him. We were now nose to nose. "I have wanted to be inside you since I was fifteen," he whispered.

"I was married," I whispered back.

"Not now!"

My knees started to wobble and all I could say was, "Too old."

"I am not!" He teased. We both smiled. Then we kissed. Slow soft, sweet. And way too long! I pulled away. I stared into his face and saw the sadness in his eyes.

"I'm sorry," he said. "I shouldn't have assumed."

"Well, I shouldn't have taken advantage," I replied. The whole situation started to feel a bit creepy. I replayed what had just happened and found myself comparing Terry's kiss with Marie's. They were related after all. What's wrong with this picture? "I gotta go." I said, backing away. "Please . . . I mean . . . thank you. For dinner and all. And the advice . . . " I continued backing up trying all the while to avoid any unseen obstacles. "I had fun! Really. And we'll talk again . . . soon"

When I reached my car I fumbled for my keys which I promptly dropped. Looking back, I could see Terry smiling sweetly. I wished he didn't look so good. Retrieving my keys, I pushed the button to unlock my door. Once inside, I took the deepest breath I had since giving birth. As I drove down the long drive, I watched Terry in my rear view mirror, standing alone, watching me leave.

"You idiot." I said out loud as I drove like a mad woman back to my mother's house. What was I thinking? Kissing Terry? It had to be the wine . . . that was it . . . two glasses of wine and I'll dance on a tabletop . . . or a face! I tried to calm myself. Maybe this was normal. Being middle-aged, single, and horny . . . or maybe I was craving attention I'd been lacking for the last ten years. But my best friend's brother?

I remember how I felt when Henry and Marie . . . Oh my god! I had totally forgotten!

My little brother and my best friend!

During Marie's first three years of marriage, she developed a polyp on one of her bronchi. Henry was doing his residency, and it made sense that she would seek his professional opinion. They began a secret affair. Both denied having sex, of course.

Marie told me, "It was spiritual." Yeah right! It almost ruined our friendship forever.

As I let myself into my mother's house, I found Manuel and my mother curled up on the couch, watching a movie. Manuel turned upon hearing me and smiled. He gestured that my mother was asleep. I don't ever remember seeing my mother and father cuddle, let alone hug one another. After Rachel's death, I'm not sure I even remember mother being affectionate with her remaining children. My mother must have felt very secure in order to fall asleep in a man's arms. Or maybe she had really lost her mind.

I felt an annoying lump in my throat as I ascended the staircase. Avoiding the emotional barrage of photos, I reached the top and stood facing the closed door to my parents' bedroom. In the couple of days I had been home, I hadn't gone into that room. The room had given me a false sense of safety when I was little. Never a good sleeper, I would creep out of my bedroom in the middle of the night and open the door to their room. Slipping quietly inside, I would sit just inside the door. I didn't want them to wake up, but I needed to see that they were there. I would watch the rise and fall of the quilt my grandma had made, knowing that they were still breathing underneath. They slept on entirely opposite sides of the bed, as if an invisible wall was keeping them from touching. I realized the last time I was in that room was just before my father died. I wasn't sure I wanted to open the door. Since it is my nature to be curious, I did. It took a few seconds to acclimate to the sight before me. Where once a four poster bed stood, there was now a sleek bed frame. A large Mexican serape was draped over the bed. The antique lamps that had been passed down from generations of Mancuso's had been replaced by Mexican pottery converted into magnificent lamps. The room that had been so familiar to me my entire life now reflected my mother's new life that I knew nothing about.

I walked over to look at the photos on the side table. There was an old photo of my father standing in front of the college, and one taken of the three of us children at the pony rides a week before Rachel died. I knew these photos. Another caught my eye. One that I had never seen before. I picked it up. It was a photo of my mother as a very young woman, maybe even a teenager. I didn't recognize the man. Obviously Hispanic, he was very handsome and had his arms around my mother. The photo had been taken somewhere in Mexico. I set it down, wondering why this photo now had center stage in my mother's bedroom.

I turned, at the sound of Manuel quietly clearing his throat. He had my sleeping mother in his arms.

"Sorry, Miss Sarah, I put your mother to her bed?"

I felt as if I was in another dimension. I nodded to Manuel and watched him gently place my mother on the bed and smooth her hair away from her face. He looked up at me and smiled. "She likes to sleep early now," he whispered.

I nodded.

He slowly walked by me and said good night.

Something struck me, "Manuel?" I asked. "Is this you?" I picked up the photo of my very young mother with the young man.

"Si, Miss Sarah. A lifetime ago." With that, he turned and walked down the stairs.

I stood in the room, holding the photo, looking down at my sleeping mother, feeling as though my heart would break. I never thought of my mother having secrets. That had been left to my father and Henry and me. Apparently, she did. I returned the photo and covered my mother with a blanket. Looking down at her, I was thrust back to a day when I was ten years old.

When I returned from school, I thought I was the only one in the house as my brother had Pop Warner, my father was at work, and my mother always had her hair done on Tuesdays. I was more than a surprised when I bolted up the stairs and found the door to my parents' room open. My mother was lying prone on the bed. I assumed she wasn't feeling well, because she never missed going to the salon if for no other reason than to hear the latest gossip. I crept into her room and reached the edge of the bed. Something was wrong. My mother's mouth was wide open, and she was pasty looking. Her mascara had run down her face making a macabre Rorschach pattern. Then I spotted the empty pill bottles on the bed next to her. My mother's pill consumption had increased after Rachel's death, but it was clear to me that what she had done was not by prescription.

"Mom?" I said loudly. There was no response. "MOM?" I was louder this time, and I threw in a few shakes of her body. Still no response. So I did what any quick thinking ten-year-old would do . . . I slapped her really hard in the face.

A slight moan escaped from her mouth. Relieved, I hit her again, and this time she stirred even more.

I ran into the bathroom, grabbed the waste paper basket, and set it beside the bed. Then I jumped on the bed next to her and pulled and pushed my mother as hard as I could over to the edge of the bed.

"Whhhaaa arrr??" Her eyes flickered open briefly then closed.

I proceeded to do what I had seen my mother do to Henry after he had eaten too many chewable aspirin. I pried her mouth open and stuck my little fingers down her throat. She began coughing and spewing and thrashing her arms at me. Within seconds, things I never thought possible came up and out of her mouth. She heaved up what looked like her entire insides. When she became unresponsive I grabbed her arms and tried to get her off the bed. She tried to fight me off. "Mom, come to the bathroom," I said as I struggled to drag her across the floor by her armpits. I finally got her to the toilet where instinctively she dropped to her knees, as if in prayer, facing the bowl. When she began to retch again, I ran to get the phone. We always kept emergency numbers neatly typed next to the phones. I grabbed the list and pulled the phone next to her just in time to see her lose consciousness.

I dialed the fire department as fast as my fingers would allow. I hoped my grandpa Reginald would be on duty.

When I heard the sirens blaring up our driveway and saw my grandpa behind the wheel, I ran full tilt into his arms and cried like a baby, sobbing and pointing up the stairs. Whatever semblance of control I had was totally lost in my grandfather's arms.

In my teenage years, I learned that my mother had discovered that my father had begun an affair shortly after Rachel's death. He had taken a job teaching an adult class at night and had met a nurse. As angry as I was with my father for his betrayal of all of us somewhere, down deep, I understood it. My mother had become cold and calculating. Each time she took another handful of pills, it was a form of blackmail. I was the unlucky one who always discovered her . . . and saved her. The same routine would play out each time with my father sobbing at her hospital bedside. I would try to keep Henry distracted. Without realizing it, I gradually began to squelch all pain and almost all my emotions.

• • •

I was around the same age as my mother had been at the time of these episodes. Having had my own experiences with a cheating spouse, I developed sympathy for my mother. As I stared down at her peaceful, sleeping face, I surprised myself with an emotion I was not used to feeling. A sincere love for her.

Switching off the light at the door, I found Manuel waiting for me in the hall. He was holding a box that he handed to me.

"Miss Sarah, I think you should have these things . . . " He looked as if he had been crying. I took the box and thanked him.

I flipped on the overhead light in my room and placed the box on the bed. I really wasn't up for finding out what piece of the past it held. All of a sudden, something hit the window and then again. Looking out I was surprised to see Terry in the driveway tossing pebbles. I opened the latch and raised the glass.

"Hello Terry . . . What are you doing?"

"Come down, and I'll explain!" he answered. I had a smile on my face as I skipped down the stairs. Once outside, I found a very contrite young man.

"Sarah!" he said, kicking a stray pebble from under his foot.

"Terry!" I answered back.

"I don't know if I can apologize enough for . . . well, forcing myself on you and . . . "

"Forcing yourself?" I cut him off. "You didn't do anything of the kind, Terry." I hooked my arm through his and guided him down the pathway leading to the little pond out back. "I'm a grown woman. I certainly wouldn't let something happen to me unless I was a willing participant." As we walked, I sensed that he began to relax a little.

"When I was little, I remember so distinctly how I felt about you." Terry said. "You were the model girl. I ended up comparing every future girlfriend to you. Maybe I found the closeness you had with my sister intriguing . . . I don't know. Anyway, when I saw you a few nights ago, after not seeing you in years, it triggered something in me, and I just couldn't help myself."

We stopped just shy of the pond. Several bullfrogs called out for perspective mates. I took a deep breath, and looked at Terry square in the face. "Terry, you are a magnificent young man. I enjoyed the kiss we shared . . . maybe too much . . . but the truth is you are Marie's baby brother and I am much older than you. The whole thing is just way too complicated for me. But that doesn't mean that I don't love the way you look, the way you kiss . . . it's just . . . "

"Got it!" he interrupted. "I just really wanted to say that I was sorry, that's all. Although I'm not really sorry, if truth be known. At least I got the kiss I have dreamed of for the last twenty years!"

The two of us started to laugh. We laughed so hard that we had to hold each other up. As we calmed down, we smiled warmly at each other. We walked arm in arm to the front of the house. When we rounded the corner, the hair on my neck stood to full attention as I realized my mother was standing in the doorway in her nightgown.

"Rachel?" she called into the night air.

"No, Mama, it's Sarah," I responded.

"How dare you stay out this late, Rachel? What in the world are you thinking?" She raised her voice. I felt my body collapse slightly against Terry. "I have to go." I said, apologizing to him.

"I know, but we should talk soon about all of this." I kissed him on the cheek and thanked him for his frankness and walked over to my mother.

"Mama, let's get you to bed," I said as I looped my arm through hers.

"Rachel, Rachel, Rachel . . . " she continued, "Don't you know how upset your father would be if he knew you were out with some boy?"

"I know, Mama" I replied as I led her back up the stairs.

"You are his favorite, you know . . . " she confided.

"I know . . . Mother . . . I know," I said, feeling how sad this was becoming.

Once upstairs, I guided her back toward her bed. She pulled back the covers and climbed in. I tucked her in snugly. She looked up at me and said "You are a great daughter, Rachel. One that a parent will always be proud of." She turned her back, plumped her pillow and that was it. No more conversation . . . done.

I bit my lip in a feeble attempt not to sob. When had all this happened? When did dementia start taking over my mother? And what could I do about it? I backed out of her room as quietly as I could, and made my way into my own room, where I plopped on my bed. I put my head into my hands feeling as if I might implode. Instead, I got up and opened my laptop to check my e-mails. I had four. The first was from Phoebe, my older girl.

"Hey, Ma . . . hope it's going alright. Call me. Need to speak with you regarding life changing decisions I am making. Spoke to Dad already, and he's on board . . . love ya, P."

"Oh Christ," I thought, "what on earth could this mean?" Last time Phoebe made a "life changing decision" it involved a stripper pole and a tongue piercing.

My second e-mail was from my publisher: "Sarah dahling . . . love the pages . . . keep it up . . . so to speak . . . LOL!!! Just had an offer from Playboy channel to make "Lust in L. A." a TV movie!!! Will let you know! Love and xxxxx's Sybil"

Ewwwwwuuuu . . . Playboy Channel?? Doesn't Spielberg read trashy novels? I could write Jaws meets Deep Throat only the shark won't have teeth! I'm flexible!

My next message was from Lily, my baby . . . "Mama . . . I miss you so much. I am having a blast at school though. My sociology professor is unbelievable, and all the pre-med is uber challenging. How's Nana? I was thinking of coming up there for Thanksgiving? Love you ooodles and ooodles . . . LILY!!!xoxoxoxoxox "

Oy! Thanksgiving!? I hadn't even realized that it was coming up and I hadn't even begun to think about it. I used to be so on top of the holidays when the kids were little. I had one area of the garage dedicated to Halloween, Thanksgiving, Christmas, and Easter! The front lawn always looked like Walt Disney and Martha Stewart had mated.

I didn't even want to open the fourth e-mail when I saw it was from Brad. Opening his e-mails was like opening up a can of worms . . . maggots even. He still knew how to push my buttons. Now that he was banging someone else, I didn't feel the need to subject myself to his manipulations that cause my angina.

I needed to get some sleep, and whatever he had to say could wait until the morning. I closed my laptop and began to undress. To bathe or not to bathe, that was the question. I've always loved a bath, especially before bed. The submersion of my body into a lovely pool of warm water brought on the most blissful, tranquil feeling. I read somewhere that a girl who positioned her vagina just below the tap's running water was guaranteed the ultimate experience! I must have wasted most of the world's supply of water, trying to achieve that ultimate experience she spoke of. Never happened for me. However, it became a chapter in *The Bitches Brew*.

Maryann arrived in London, on a typical, rainy October evening around six p.m. She had arranged a longer layover as her college roommate, Liza, now lived there and she wanted to spend some time with her.

Liza had worked as a flight attendant too, but for different airlines. They didn't see one another that much anymore.

Maryann loved the sounds of the English taxi cabs. They always sounded as if they might fall apart.

The cab pulled up outside Liza's flat off Kensington High Street. Maryann texted her friend that she had arrived, and was on the street below. She paid her driver, and saw the front door fly open. Liza stood there grinning from ear to ear.

Maryann didn't even open her umbrella, she just ran up the stairs and into her friend's arms.

After the Indian take-out and a lot of wine and catching up, Liza said she would run Maryann a nice bath. Maryann sat by the toasty fire and began smelling lovely scents wafting through the air from the bathroom. She could make out Lavender and orange. She walked into Liza's bathroom to find lit candles, another bottle of wine, two wine glasses and tons of bubbles in her sunken tub.

"Wow! Is this for me?" Maryann laughed.

"Well, that is if you don't want company?" Liza replied. Maryann and Liza had fooled around in college. Where Maryann preferred men, Liza stuck with women.

Feeling the effects of wine they began to disrobe. Maryann got into the tub first. The water was perfect and the scented candles and the bath salts made a lovely aphrodisiac. Liza got into the tub and laid her body back in Maryann's arms. Maryann wrapped her arms around Liza. They talked a bit more, and then Maryann began stroking Liza's breasts. "I don't remember your breasts as being as lovely as they are now," she teased.

"Well, you haven't touched them in years, my dear."

Liza turned to face Maryann.

"You're the only woman I have ever been with, you know?" Maryann said.

"Well, you're not the only woman I've ever been with!" And Liza kissed her friend hard and passionately.

"I can tell you only kiss men!" Liza laughed.

"How can you tell that?"

"Just can!"

Maryann, always up for a challenge, grabbed Liza's face and plunged her tongue deep into her mouth. "Mmmmm, that's more like it," Liza moaned, "I'm going to show you something special." She took the hand held shower in her hands and turned it on. There was a dial at the top for varying degrees of massage pressure. Liza turned it to the pulsating setting.

"Lie back my dear, and I am going to take you to new heights."

Liza aimed the shower massage directly on Maryann's hungry pussy.

• • •

I was way too restless, even for a bath. I decided to check the e-mail from my Rottweiler ex-husband. We had barely spoken since our separation, unless it was about the kids. I could never take him seriously after I found him with that spray-tanned, mall rat.

• • •

I was in my car, running late, on my way to my agent's office. It was raining a heavy, torrential rain, the kind of rain Los Angeles isn't known for. I was concentrating hard on the road when my phone rang. After the news broke regarding cell phone use and brain tumors, the hypochondriac in me had kicked in. I immediately went out and got a hands-free thingamagig. Of course, the thingamagig had fallen between the seat and the armrest, and I was groping around trying to find it. As I was placing it in my ear, I could already hear Brad talking but it wasn't to me. He must have pushed the redial button on his office phone and did not realize we were connected. I did what any trusting, loving wife would do. I didn't speak . . . I just listened.

"I want a dozen red roses sent upstairs to her office along with a venti soy latte. Suite 204." Brad's voice was determined, strong and sexy. "No, just bill me as usual."

In that moment, my life fell apart. I made a Mario Andretti 180 in the rain and headed for my husband's office.

I actually sat in my car for more than an hour, staring at the window on the first floor. I wondered how I would confront him. What would I say? What could I say? Finally, I mustered up the courage to take myself to his office. "Fuck the umbrella," I decided as I ran full tilt toward the glass doors. I must have looked like a drowned rat, upon entering.

"Sarah! Nice to see you." Sidney, the security guard, greeted me as I rushed in.

"You too, Sid!" I tried to hide the fact that my heart was about to jump out of my chest like *Alien* and plaster itself onto his face.

When I got into the elevator, I thought I might puke. What had I just heard? Was I overreacting? Was I totally crazy? Had I misinterpreted what I heard? Brad works so hard that he doesn't have time for his family. When could he possibly have time for an affair?

As I neared his closed office door, I knew. What I didn't anticipate was what was on the other side of the door. Brad's assistant had left for the day, so I was able to open the door to his office quietly. Brad's Armani trousers were sitting on top of his Bruno Magli's, and he was thrusting his trusty six inch into the plump behind of suite 204. I never did appreciate being fucked from behind, but seeing suite 204 spread over the top of Brad's desk and hearing the moan escape her cupid's mouth, I wondered if I had been missing out. He was holding on to 204's hips as if she might actually fly across the room if he didn't. Then he caught sight of me from the corner of his eye. Without acknowledging me he took his hands off bitchfacecuntwhore's hips and made a fist just under her breastbone. He feigned doing the Heimlich maneuver.

"Come on dammit," he said "You can do it!!" He looked at me straight in the eye and said without blinking "Chicken bone!!" He continued to pump blondie's chest.

Very resourceful, I thought. Nice try!

204 was coughing wildly by this point.

"I am saving her life!!" He yelled out to me.

As I turned to leave, 204 exclaimed, "What the fuck? You tryin' to kill me or somethin'?"

I headed home through the rain and called a locksmith on the way. The one time I wished I had passed out I didn't! One thing I was sure of, the locks would be changed before my soon to be exhusband got home.

Chapter Five

Til Death . . . Blah, Blah, Blah

It was the spring of my senior year in college. Marie had been correct about my unexpected hurling, the morning of her wedding. I was pregnant. Aside from the round the clock vomiting, morning sickness my ass. I threw up every hour on the hour. I had huge veins all over my breasts and chest that were a lovely shade of indigo. I finally got myself to the doctor. Although he took my blood to be certain, he was convinced I was pregnant as well.

Brad was still in law school, and I was barely twenty. We weren't even living together, but the thought of an abortion never entered my mind. I had many friends who had had abortions and said it was no big deal. I was all for Roe v Wade, but I just couldn't do it. To my surprise, Brad just said, "What's the big deal? We'll get married."

"You mean I don't have to go into a home with other unwed mothers and have my parents disown me and be ostracized by my friends?" I sobbed.

Brad shook his head and smiled. "Of course not honey. It's what we both want some day anyway. It came a little earlier than we planned. Just do me a favor. Don't say anything to our parents."

"Never crossed my mind!" I promised. Honestly, how was it possible? I had obviously found the greatest man on earth!

We planned the wedding really fast because I was already beginning my second trimester. My mother kept asking for me to wait and have a summer wedding. We lied and said that Brad would be interning at a firm that summer and that it would be too stressful. He was going to meet with a firm, which was the truth, but he had no clue what would happen. Luckily Brad's mother was all aboard for late spring. She wanted to have the wedding in her lovely garden in Pasadena.

Marie helped with everything, thank God, including what I should wear that would hide any signs of what was going on underneath the dress. It was an off the shoulder, empire dress in French lace. I wore flowers in my hair like the flowerchild I once aspired to be. Brad wore his father's tuxedo. My parents flew down with my brother Henry. As I waited in my gown in the master bedroom, there was a knock at the door. It was my father. He would be walking me down the aisle. I saw a sadness in him as he stood there.

"Daddy, are you alright?"

"You'll never dance on the table tops in Monte Carlo."

"I'm sorry, Dad. I don't know what that means."

He looked deeply into my eyes. "You are so young to be getting married. You should have a whole life before you begin this one." He glanced at the floor. "I'm sorry I shouldn't be saying this on your wedding day."

I told him that I loved him for it, but I was certain I was doing the right thing. I cupped his face in my hands and promised to dance on a tabletop in Monte Carlo.

He took my hand and squeezed it. He told me he was pleased to be able to walk, at least one of his daughters, down the aisle. I took it as a compliment. Although I knew the ghost of Rachel loomed over us all that day. It wasn't until years later that I realized he had been talking about his own experiences. We were later to discover around this time that my dad was having another affair.

It was swelteringly hot that day, which became my excuse for being sick in Marjorie's rose bushes. "Poor Sarah . . . she's so nervous . . . and it is sooo hot today!!" I heard people saying.

Underneath the rose covered arbor, looking into Brad's loving eyes, I felt like the luckiest woman in the world. The celebration was nothing but the best. People asked when we would be having children. I told them as soon as possible.

An hour into the reception, Marie took my hand and led me into the house. "I need to talk to you," she said.

We entered the powder room on the lower level. I had a Pavlovian response whenever I saw a toilet. I was instantly nauseated. "Do we have to be in a bathroom?"

"Oh my God, fine!" Marie was annoyed.

"No. It's alright. Don't worry," I responded, "I'll just hurl into the solid gold swan fauceted sink if I have to."

"This is serious." Marie took my hands in hers.

"What? What is it?" I asked.

"Last week," she began, "I got home early, and to my surprise, I saw David's car in the driveway." Marie's eyes began to tear.

"Oh God, Marie . . . don't tell me. Another woman?"

She shook her head.

"A . . . man?" I whispered.

"No, nothing like that."

I just waited for her to tell me.

"I went into our bedroom. He was standing in front of the mirror . . . in my bra and panties!"

Okay . . . strike me dead . . . A laugh surfaced from the bottom of my stomach to my mouth. I couldn't contain my laughter.

"It's not funny!" Marie was offended.

"Oh God, Marie . . . I know!" I propped myself up on the sink for fear I would laugh so hard I'd hit the ground. Then something remarkable happened, maybe because of our love for one another and the deep understanding we shared. Marie began to laugh, too. The two of us hung on to one another for dear life, tears running down our cheeks as both of us tried to catch our breath. After several minutes, we just stood, totally winded, staring at one another. Finally, I asked, "What are you going to do?"

"What do you mean?"

"Are you going to leave him?" I asked.

"Of course not!" She replied indignantly.

"Well, good!" I couldn't come up with anything else to say.

Marie explained that no one knew, and even David hadn't seen her see him. "So he has a little quirkiness," she shrugged. "I still love him."

"Good!" I said again. I was beginning to feel like a puppet with my head bobbing up and down. I was also wondering how much she was lying about her feelings.

"But hey, it's your wedding day for cryin' out loud. Let's party!" Marie grabbed my arm and led me back outside.

It was dusk and the scent of night blooming jasmine was wafting through the warm air. A lovely string quartet was playing Bach or Mozart. I didn't have a clue. Tiny tea lights had been placed around the property and some even floated in the Olympic sized pool. I caught Brad's eye as I walked toward him. Everyone seemed to stop in that moment as the two of us made our way toward each other. It was all very romantic, until I found myself fighting another tsunami of nausea. He steered me to a private spot. In those days Brad thought that everything I did was adorable. Even my throwing up in his mother's yard made him smile. I could not have loved him more.

At two in the morning March 14, 1976, I woke up thinking I had wet the bed. So I waddled into the bathroom and sat on the toilet to have a lovely pee. As I wiped myself, I realized that the fluid I had felt before was not urine.

"Brad." I tapped him lightly. "Brad, wake up. My water broke."

And from the deepest, darkest sleep, my husband was suddenly airborne. He shot out of bed as if I had stuck dynamite up his ass.

"Honey, I'm fine. Slow down," I tried to reassure him.

He was on a mission. Trying to find his keys, trying to locate the suitcase I had packed. All the while he repeated, "It's two weeks early. What does that mean?"

I just told him we needed to go quickly and safely to the hospital. It would all be fine. Until that point I hadn't really felt anything other than slimy fluid down my legs. As soon as we got into the car, the contractions started. The enlightened love child in me was all about natural birth. I wanted to do it at home in a bathtub. Since my mother almost had a heart attack when I told her my plans, I agreed that my first child would be delivered in an antiseptic, brightly lit hospital.

We pulled into the emergency entrance, and Brad ran inside. A nurse soon came out wheeling a chair. I was surprised that my contractions were coming every two minutes and were so power-ful I thought my insides would explode. I was trying desperately to remember all the breathing techniques I had learned at the few birthing classes we managed to attend. All I could do was moan, which prompted Brad to remind me to breathe, which prompted me to tell him to tell him to fuck off. You don't mess with a woman in labor! The nurse began shoving paper work at me, even though I was telling her that I thought I had to push.

"Isn't this your first child? How long have you been in labor?" she asked without much sympathy to my cries.

"My whole life!" I screamed at her.

"Well, then. We aren't going to get very far if we have that kind of attitude are we?" She smirked.

"No, we will be a dead nurse if we don't check me immediately," I yelled. Brad had disappeared, and I hadn't the foggiest idea where he had gone.

Psycho nurse wheeled me into a room and told me to get onto the bed. I tried to maneuver my body onto what seemed like the bed from *The Princess and the Pea*. I knew it couldn't have been as high as

I thought it was, but I had never tried to mount anything with what felt like a bowling ball about to drop out from between my legs.

"Okay, Missy. Let's see what all the fuss is about," the nurse said as she pulled up my muumuu.

"Oh my God. You're crowning!"

"Does that have anything to do with you being a royal pain in the ass?" I hissed through my teeth.

Phoebe Elizabeth was born ten minutes later with neither my doctor nor my husband present. Nurse Ratchett delivered her with a couple attendings standing by.

"It's a girl," Nurse said as I heard my baby cry.

"Far out!" I replied. I had never used that phrase before or since. Why I channeled John Denver I will never know. As Phoebe was placed in my arms, I knew the true meaning of love. Even nurse Ratchett and I smiled at one another.

It turned out that Brad had gone to make the perfunctory phone calls. Of course, his parents were first. They lived in the same city, I'll give him that, and my parents were still up north expecting me not to go into labor this soon. When Brad returned, I had a newborn at my breast. Brad broke down and sobbed.

"I missed everything!" he wailed. "My first child. I can't believe it!!"

At that moment, I thought to myself why am I not feeling sorry for him? He was making this all about him. He never asked how I was or what I had just gone through. It was all about his missing it!

"What were you doing?" I asked.

"I was making the phone calls. All the people on your list, for crying out loud!" "Maybe you could have waited until after she was born?" I was smiling. I didn't get mad. A kind of euphoria takes place after delivery. I know that it has to do with hormones. Oxytosin. Something else kicks in, too. The meaning of life! All of a sudden, you realize how powerful it is to be a woman. You know that you would dive under a moving train for this person swaddled in your arms. Nothing else really matters.

We were home in two days. Brad went home the night after Phoebe was born and set up her crib. He complained bitterly about how badly he had thrown his back out doing so. My mother flew down to help and stayed in our bed with me, because Brad insisted on taking the couch.

"Why Phoebe?" my mother asked at the two a.m. feeding my first night home.

"Why not?" I replied.

My mother sighed. "Well, I guess I thought you might name your daughter after Rachel?"

I searched my mother's face for some sort of sign that could help me with this one. "Are we Jewish and you never told me?" I asked.

"What's that supposed to mean?" She snorted.

"Well, our family has never named people after the dead," I said.

My mother's lip quivered a bit. And I wondered if this might be the second time in my life I would see her cry. But no, she bit her bottom lip and willed the tears away. "Mother." I took her hand. "No one can replace Rachel, and Rachel had her own name. I wouldn't want anyone to take her place, even symbolically."

My mother sighed again and scooted down under the blankets. "I understand," she said, turning her back on me and feigning sleep.

I looked down at my child attached to my breast. What a satisfying feeling it is to nurse your child. I swore to her in that I would always communicate with her the best way that I knew how.

Within a few weeks, the overly generous, unselfish, un- egotistical man for whom I had recited my wedding vow regressed into the equivalent of a two-year-old. He wanted all of my attention as though I was his mother, not Phoebe's. At first it was subtle, but it soon became more obvious. He stared at my breasts as I would open my shirt to nurse. Granted, my breasts were the size of silos and my nipples looked like Oscar Meyer Bologna. I understood the fascination. When he began to drill me about the breastfeeding, I realized there was more going on with him. "Can't she take a bottle yet? When will your boobs be normal again? How much milk does one baby need, for Christ's sake?"

Phoebe was three months old when I stopped nursing. I really didn't want to stop. In fact, I think I might still be nursing my kids if it wasn't taboo. And knock me down if it didn't seem like a conspiracy. My mother jumped on the bandwagon and told me how pleased she was that I would be able to concentrate more on Brad now that I had stopped breast-feeding!

"A man needs to know that he is still number one, sweetie," she pointed out.

Of course, my mother never even attempted to breast feed her children. I even saw a photo of her around eight months pregnant with me with a martini in one hand and a cigarette in the other. Talk about a generation gap.

Motherhood was all-consuming at that point. All I wanted to do was look at this gorgeous being, whom I helped create, and let the world go by. Once the decision was made to let my milk dry up, no one tells you how painful that is. I had to find other stimuli. Now that Brad was a junior partner in a law firm and barely home, I kept up a dialogue with Marie. In a weirdly symbiotic way, she had a baby too. Born three months after Phoebe. He weighed in at eight pounds and was a C-section. Marie's stomach looked great. My baby was six pounds, and I was sure my vagina and my stomach would never be the same.

Marie suggested I pick up my writing again. "Even if you never do anything with it, you are a good writer Sarah, and it will give you an outlet," she preached. Were we really this smart at the age of twenty?

We talked at least once a week. Mostly about our babies and sometimes about our spouses and how uninvolved with us they seemed, now that we were mothers. We never spoke about what she had revealed to me on my wedding day.

I launched myself into the career I still have to this day. I'm not really sure why or how I fell into the erotic romance genre, seeing as I hadn't really experienced any of that myself. I had been considered a fairly good poet, so why wasn't I channeling Emily Dickenson instead of Harold Robbins? Beats me.

I completed my first novel *Love and Lust at Midnight* within a year, and I was damn proud. Brad was as supportive as he could be. I don't think he actually believed anything would come of this newfound hobby of mine. Brad referred to it as sexy fluff. One day after reading the cover of a paperback romance novel, I wrote down the publishing company's name. What the hell? Why not submit my manuscript to them? Months went by, and I suspected Brad was secretly pleased that I hadn't heard anything.

We celebrated Phoebe's first birthday. She took her first steps . . . they were toward the vodka-laced punch bowl. Maybe I should've known then and there she would be in and out of rehab. Brad was made partner at Korsen, Korsen, Korsen and Hertz. One day, I received a certified letter.

"Dear Miss O'Malley,

"We are pleased to inform you that we would like to publish your debut novel *Love and Lust at Midnight*.

Please contact us at your earliest convenience . . .

I don't think I actually finished the letter. I just screamed. I received a $5000 advance, and they wanted an option on my next novel.

The first thing I did was get a new typewriter. I wasn't very fast at typing, so I enrolled in a night class in order to perfect my much-needed skill. Brad took rolls of photographs of me in our back yard for the author photo. The publishers picked a shot in which I was looking off to the left and slightly upwards. It wasn't one I particularly liked. It looked as though I was wishing on a star, or something to that effect. Maybe I was?

The actual cover of the book, I learned, was typical, in those days. It was a painting, but looked very realistic. A hunky, shirtless man in polo pants and boots, holding a young raven haired girl in his arms. Her flowy dress was falling off of her shoulders. A huge horse rearing up in the background.

Over the years my book covers remained somewhat alike. Most were actual photographs of the hunk and damsel scenario. And my author photos got better and better.

It took about nine months before *Love and Lust* was published. With all the editorial notes, proofreading the galleys, sending back all the corrections, the time flew by. I was interviewed for *Publishers Weekly* as a hot, new, genre writer. Brad was still skeptical about the whole thing and concerned about how legitimate the publisher was. I felt he was just jealous that attention was being paid to me.

I signed with my first literary agent. He had seen my article in *Publishers Weekly* and had offered to represent me. My publisher made sure the book was in all the special promotions. I'm sure the exotic cover was appealing to most women. Also, it didn't hurt that several top selling authors, Tina Mason, Walter O'Rielly, Samantha Davis, had given us blurbs, on the back cover.

Brad and I bought our first home in the San Fernando Valley. Van Nuys to be exact. We found an affordable home on a quiet street. Yes, the house had a white picket fence. That is what sold it for me. I didn't really care about anything other than that fence. It signified so much.

My mother hated the house. Mainly, she hated the valley. "It's so hot here!" Yet still she was determined to line every single drawer with sweet smelling liners and color coordinated anything that was to be hung.

Not long after our move, Brad's father became ill, and Brad retreated into himself and his work, big time. It's not as if Steve and Brad were ever that close. In fact, Brad could hardly remember his dad being around when he was young. Nevertheless, Brad was devastated by the news. I decided that it would be a good time to take a trip with Phoebe, and see Marie on Nantucket. Neither of us had seen each other's children, other than photographs, and we felt it was time.

I couldn't get over the size of Marie's home; it was a beautiful colonial on an acre of lush land, five bedrooms, three baths and wrap around porches on each floor. The kitchen was decorated in provincial blues and whites. The granite counter tops, flecked with gold, sparkled in the afternoon light that poured through the large bay window above the stainless steel sinks. All the important rooms had views of the water where a small sail boat was bobbing.

"Did you order the cute boat for me?" I asked Marie on our tour of the house.

"Of course I did," she giggled. "Only the best for my best friend!"

It was great to spend time with Marie even though we knew the visit would be short. Her cross-dressing husband wasn't around much, which was probably a good thing since I'm sure I wouldn't have been able to keep my mouth shut for long. Marie had hired an au pair from Sweden. We actually could leave our children and go out to lunch or just sit with a bottle of wine in her garden looking out at the surf.

We were different now. When I tried to broach the subject of our "teen experience" and what we had done the night before her wedding, Marie behaved as though she didn't recall. Without going any deeper, I understood that she had decided it wasn't anything she wanted to stir up now that she was married and a parent. I have always wondered if maybe we hadn't short changed ourselves.

Marie's phone rang at two a.m. I figured it was for David. When Marie slipped into my room, I could read the expression on her face. Brad had told me he didn't think his father had more than twenty-four hours left. Phoebe and I took the first plane off Nantucket that morning. We would have one stop before getting into LAX. Phoebe and I would've only stayed another day anyway. Marie cried as she waved good-bye, and we swore to call once a month without fail. I didn't see Marie again for ten years.

Brad's father, having suffered a major heart attack was not expected to make it through the night that Phoebe and I returned home. Our neighbor, Susan, a twenty-four-year-old nursing student, said she'd be happy to watch Phoebe while I went to the hospital where Brad had been sitting vigil.

The look on my mother-in-law's face as I walked into the hospital room was not welcoming. Brad's mother had a way of making people who weren't immediate family feel as if they had not bathed in a while. She would scrunch up her face, purse her lips, and look as if she was smelling rotten air. Even with her husband in critical condition she was dressed in a Chanel suit with a strand of good pearls around her neck. God forbid she walk out of her house looking less than perfect. I felt as though I was invading a family sanctuary. I was definitely the outsider. Brad, who was sitting in a chair close to his father looked up and smiled. Steve was lying so still in the bed, his mouth wide open and his breathing labored. I had never seen anyone close to death before.

"Hi, Honey," Brad whispered as he walked over to me, "I'm glad you came." He kissed me tenderly on the cheek, and I saw Marjorie's expression soften at that point.

Brad suggested we walk to the cafeteria where we could talk without disturbing his dad.

We sat across from one another for several minutes without saying a word. Brad's blue eyes were streaked red from all the crying he had been doing. "So, how's the baby?" He finally asked.

"She's great. A little tired. It was harder on the plane this time. She just didn't want to sleep, and now that she's walking, that's all she wants to do . . . "

I could see that Brad really wasn't paying attention. I felt that I was really rambling on about nothing. We continued to sit, warming our hands around the Styrofoam coffee cups.

I didn't go back into Steve's room. Brad said he'd call if anything happened. It was after midnight, and I didn't want to leave the baby any longer. I got into my car and sat for a while staring up at all the lights in the hospital. I tried to imagine how many women were giving birth to new life at that moment and how many lives would end tonight. I never saw my father-in-law alive again.

Brad came home around five a.m. and went straight to the kitchen. I got up when I heard him rummaging through the cupboards. He was standing in the middle of the kitchen with all the drawers and cupboards open. He had a box of cereal in one hand and a carton of eggs in the other. He looked as if he was in a standing eight count, and he would be face down in the ring any minute.

"Honey?"

He looked at me as if he didn't recognize me. I could tell he had been drinking. "I can't decide if I want cereal or eggs." He held up both.

I walked over to him and took the box of cereal from one hand and the eggs from the other and set them down behind me. I put my arms around my husband who began to tremble. The two of us sank to the floor, and Brad began to sob. We held one another for what seemed like hours. My nightgown was soaked with both of our tears.

And then Brad spoke. "I never told my dad I love him."

Brad broke away from our embrace. He went upstairs and into the bathroom. I heard the shower. Within the hour, he appeared, clean and shaven, a new man. He put on one of his finer suits and went to the office. It was the first and possibly the last time I would see him cry.

Our lives changed dramatically during the next few years. We bought another house, this time in the Brentwood area that was great for entertaining Brad's colleagues and their wives. We were definitely movin' up in the world. Phoebe was eight and going to a very good elementary school. I entertained Brad's colleagues and their wives regularly. I published a second novel and had begun another. I had a substantial contract to write a third. I discovered to my delight, I was pregnant again.

Brad and I had been trying to have another baby for a long time, then gave up. We weren't having a lot of sex in those days. I figured it must have been that quickie mutual shower, before he went to work one morning that did it. Brad was thrilled when I told him. Of

course, he was planning for a son. We told Phoebe after my first trimester. My belly was already popping a bit, and I was feeling terrific.
Phoebe would touch my stomach, close her eyes and pray for a girl!

Marjorie, my ever-present mother-in-law, had a date and a place
picked out for the baby shower. Just as I went into my fifth month, I
started to bleed. The ultrasound showed a baby without a heartbeat.
My world crashed in on me. I couldn't believe it. I didn't have any
symptoms. I had done everything right.

"These things just happen sometimes. Usually there is a reason
and it winds up being for the best," my doctor tried to explain.

Nothing could take away the pain and the grief I felt. He offered
me the choice of letting the baby miscarry on its own or his removing it. I chose the latter. I couldn't bear the idea of having to wait as
long as two weeks and holding on to my now deceased baby.

During the next few months, I couldn't pull myself out of the
depression. Brad seemed oddly relieved by what had happened. He
behaved as though I had just suffered a bad cold. Now that it was
over with, he expected me to just move on. I hated him for not crying with me. I hated that he wouldn't allow me to talk truthfully to
Phoebe. And I hated that he seemed to disappear even more into
his work. I ended up turning to my writing and began to travel to
do research. We hired a house keeper who also helped with Phoebe.
Before long, we became a typical middle of the road, American family,
God help us.

Chapter Six

What Lies Beneath

Sitting on the sofa bed in what had become my father's office, I thought about Brad's e-mail. His heads up about Phoebe's life crisis was highly supportive. It was about time he was supportive. I closed the laptop and decided to try to sleep. Sleep was usually elusive for me. Most of the time I would lay staring at the ceiling, wanting to weep with exhaustion, but I dropped off without a problem.

The next morning started off cloudy. My room was still fairly dark when I awoke. I could smell wonderful aromas wafting up from the kitchen. I could make out bacon and coffee, but the other smells were a mystery. Wrapping a robe around myself, I ventured down to investigate. My mother was in one of her jogging suits with her hair in a chignon. She was wearing a sheer lipstick stain that matched the color of her high cheekbones. She looked beautiful.

"Hello, my darling." She beamed. "I have made a lovely breakfast."

"It smells wonderful, Mother," I said as I took a seat in the little nook. I searched my memory for the last time I could remember her doing any sort of cooking, and I couldn't recall. This morning, there were scrambled eggs with bacon, home fries and pumpkin pancakes!

She poured me a cup of fresh coffee and sat down with her second cup. I felt as though I hadn't eaten for years. I began wolfing down the food like a convict. "Where did you learn to make these pancakes Mother? They are amazing!" I said with a mouth full.

"The Food Network!" she answered. "I'm going to go for a run soon, and then I have a doctor's appointment."

I asked her which doctor and she told me it was Dr. Dreayer, who had been the family doctor for years. I suggested that I join her, and she nodded

"That would be fine, dear. If you really want to." Then she took off.

I watched, through the window, as she bolted down the driveway in a full trot. I don't think I had ever known my mother to exercise in her life. I scraped the last bit of food from my plate, washed it, and put it in the drainer by the sink. I walked out the back door toward my mother's garden. The air reminded me of being in London about the time when Phoebe was six.

I was writing a book called *The Cock and Bull* about a young exchange student living with an English family over a summer. It had occurred to me that if I wrote about a certain location I would have to travel there for research! Light bulb moment! I had a series of wonderful adventures in exotic locations. Paris, Cannes, Hawaii. Madrid. I would spend up to three weeks away at times. London was one of my favorite cities. It was the first time I had left Brad or Phoebe for any length of time. With the help in place, I was confident that I would return to find everything as it was before I left. The London air always seemed crisp and thick. After each rain, which was a common occurrence, a smell rose up from the concrete. A mildewy, acrid, muddy smell. I loved it. My skin never looked better. I stayed in a charming, small hotel near Hyde Park in Kensington and became instantly addicted to Indian food and Smarties.

I walked down the High Street around five p.m. each evening and headed for the Taj Mahal restaurant, where I would order a Vindaloo or a Masala curry, a large piece of naan with everything smothered in lime pickle and raita. Since I wasn't having sex with anyone, only writing about people fucking, I didn't care if I had the breath of an elephant. I loved being able to pick out the English people from the tourists. I became quite good at it. It wasn't difficult. The people with huge cameras swinging from their necks were tourists and the men who wore shorts with brown ankle socks and black shoes were English.

My heroine in *The Cock and Bull* was eighteen and a college student. She had recently discovered that her parents were actually her grandparents. Her real mother had become pregnant at fifteen and left the country after having her baby. Hillary ventures to find her in England. In the meantime, she meets and falls for a bartender at the local pub, yes, The Cock and Bull, and they have a passionate affair. Simon not only had the cock, but he ended up being full of bull.

"It was all consuming," Hillary wrote in her diary. "I couldn't believe that my body was capable of doing the things that Simon was introducing me to. Shortly after closing the pub tonight, Simon picked me up, setting me on top of the bar. He grabbed my legs, and pushed them open with such force I gasped loudly. He took a large bottle of Bailey's liqueur and began rubbing the mouth of it up and down my black laced panties. He unbuttoned my shirt, pushing it aside to reveal my breasts. He poured the sweet liquid all over my tits. His tongue was hot as he licked the creamy alcohol, from my chest. Our eyes met. He licked his full lips and then parted mine with his tongue. I wasn't used to the taste of alcohol, but this tasted like chocolate candy. Then his probing fingers moved to my panties again and he slipped them off. Sliding his fingers inside me, I moaned and rocked back and forth to an intensifying beat. Pouring the last drops of the bottle onto my already wet pussy, he pressed his face between my legs. Between the slight sting of the alcohol and the friction of his stubble, I felt both pain and pleasure. I grabbed his hair causing him to thrust his tongue further into my pleasure dome and I exploded into his mouth. This was definitely a summer to remember.

Nothing much about my writing had changed. Phoebe had set up a Facebook page for me, and I knew just from that that my books had an audience, a diverse one in fact. A lot of really young women or really old. And surprisingly, truck drivers and gay men. Occasionally, I was asked to ghostwrite erotica for other novelists. And that paid well. It isn't easy writing erotica. How many times can you explain a wet pussy? Although I wasn't a recognizable celebrity I had made a decent enough name for myself that could get me into a fine restaurant in a pinch. The girls were embarrassed by my choice of career when they were young, but they think it very "cool" now. Still, it's not as if I was having these experiences in my real life. Whatever I have written, people seemed to love it. And I liked doing it!

I felt a deep sense of sadness as I stepped into my mother's garden this dewy morning. This was really the only thing my mother paid attention to after Rachel died. She loved English gardens, overgrown and beautiful. There was an area for herbs and all things roses. She knew the names of every one of them. This time of year mostly wildflowers grew here but a few roses still bloomed.

I remember hating the roses especially. I was jealous of them. One day when mother was out, Henry and I cut off all the tops of whatever flowers were blooming. It looked like a pollen apocalypse. The two of us laughed and threw petals at one another in some weird catharsis. Looking at the exquisite beauty of mother's garden I feel queasy for having been so destructive, even though I was only nine at the time.

When Olivia O'Malley got home, the day of our garden purge, I received "the belt" for the first but not last time. I was in my room when she got home. Without speaking, she came, grabbed me just underneath my armpit, and led me into her room. Closing the door with her free hand, she pushed me onto the bed. I was terrified. The look in her eyes was fierce. Opening her closet, which always smelled of baby powder, she grabbed a wide leather belt.

"Please Mommy. I am sorry," I begged. "I didn't mean it really, I didn't . . . "

Unmoved, she picked me up and forced me across her knees as she sat. As she took down my panties, she finally spoke, "You get ten of these. Anytime you behave like that again, I will increase the amount."

She began thrashing my exposed buttocks with the belt, counting out loud from one to ten. The tears that flowed from my eyes resulted from a mixture of guilt, confusion, and the sheer piercing pain of the lashing. I saw stars and I thought that I would faint.

When she finished, she pushed me away from her and told me to go clean my face. She walked into her bathroom, closed the door, and never made it to the dinner table that night.

My bottom was sore for days. I hated the fact that Henry had been exempt from the punishment, even though my mother knew he was also responsible for the devastation of the garden. To make matters worse, my father did nothing about it. I know he knew because I had overheard my parents discussing the incident.

My mother had taken him into the garden and showed him what Henry and I had done. My father asked if she had punished the two of us and she said that she had. He never asked how we were punished and she never mentioned that Henry had been excluded. I felt horribly betrayed by both my parents. I decided to write my mother a letter which I slipped under their door one night, apologizing again for what I had done. I walked around for days, feeling horrible about it. On the third day after leaving my "sorry" letter, my mother casually said, "I got your note. And I accept your apology."

I wasn't sure I felt any better, but I was glad I had made an effort.

One day when my father and I were alone in the house, I asked him why he had let Mother beat me. He genuinely looked shocked. I could read from his expression that he had no idea that it had gone that far, but he defended Mother by saying that what I did had been a horrible violation and that the punishment could've been worse. Later that evening, I heard my father yelling at mother about her hitting me. He warned her never to let that happen again. No matter what! She ignored his request, however. The next couple of times I received the belt, she told me that if I told my father she would send me to boarding school. I could never figure out how he didn't know what was happening. Looking back, I figured he must have known. He just couldn't bear it. My parents were in a constant state of denial. I was convinced that I would never trust another living soul again.

In later years I asked him why he and Mother had stayed together. "For you kids, of course," he replied.

"Good morning, Miss Sarah." I turned to see Manuel, who had on a large brimmed sombrero and a wide grin.

"Hi, Manuel."

"I was to pick some flowers for the table this morning. I think your mother will see the doctor today, no?"

I nodded my head and explained that she was out jogging and that I would be going with her to her appointment.

"That is a good thing," Manuel said as he ducked under the arbor. He began gently pruning and cutting the various plants. I watched his careful, tender hands almost caress each flower that he touched. "You see this, Miss Sarah?" He pointed to one of the roses. "It is a sterling rose. It reminds me of Miss Olivia. Striking, no?"

I looked at the delicate purple/silvery color, and I had to agree. It was a regal flower. I told Manuel that I was going to get ready to take my mother for her appointment.

As I left him still tending to garden, my heart felt like it would break. I felt alone. Even at this stage of my mother's life she was adored by this man. It hit me that I missed my father, too. He had been such a force to reckon with. Even though he became a curmudgeon as the years went by, he actually seemed to soften with Henry and me. Mother never forgave him his affairs and punished him with all her suicide attempts till he died.

When I walked into my room, the small box that Manuel had given to me the night before caught my eye. I sat down in the Lazy- boy and scanned the room. I don't think I ever really considered the room as being my father's haven. He loved to read. Not just because he had to. Maybe that was one of the reasons I turned to writing, I don't believe he ever read any of my books, but nearly all of them were in a neat line up on a top shelf. If he had ever read my work he never mentioned it.

One very late night, when I was around twelve, I remember hearing something that made me get out of bed. I walked from my room into this room and peeked inside. My father was in a fetal position, on the floor, sobbing. He had a photograph of all three of us kids next to him. I didn't know what I should do. Should I go to him and comfort him? Would he be embarrassed if he knew I had seen him like that? I watched for a few minutes and decided to go back to bed. I remember staring at the ceiling and feeling as though I had just seen someone else in that room not my own father lying there. I was numb. Over the years, I became aware that that wasn't a random incident. I heard my father crying in his study on many other occasions. I just never got out of bed again.

I began to run a bath, then sat on the edge of the bed and picked up the box. It was made of hand carved cherry wood, with an intricate inlay of Mother of Pearl on each of its sides. I hesitated before opening it, not sure what to expect. When I lifted the lid, I discovered that the entire box was filled with letters. All the envelopes were worn, and the color had bled from them. The same handwriting that I recognized as my mother's was on each. I carefully lifted out the fragile envelope on top of the pile and opened it.

December

　Darling

　Time seems to have slipped by once again. It will be Christmas next week, and I have been doing all the decorations in the house. I am sure that your church will look beautiful again this year.

　We have had a little bit of snow, which makes everything look as though it was sprinkled in sugar.

I hope that this letter finds you in good health and that we will re-unite soon.

Yours, Livvy

My hands were covered with sweat by the time I finished reading the letter. Realizing that my bath was near to overflowing I jumped to turn off the water. I slipped the letter back into its envelope and sat for a while just trying to figure it all out. I studied the address on the front. It read: Father Manuel Garcia, Church of The Angels, Mexico City, Mexico.

Father? What did that mean? Maybe my mother was writing to Manuel's father? But why would this Manuel have the box and why would my mother be calling his father, Darling?

"Sarah, I'm home," my mother called as she headed up the stairs. I quickly stashed the box under the bed. Mother stepped into the room and asked, "Shall we go down to the park and have a picnic? I was just thinking we haven't done that in so long."

"You have your doctor's appointment, Mom," I reminded her.

"Oh, fuck that," she shrugged, "it's so lovely out."

"Actually, Mother, It's supposed to rain later, and I don't think . . . " I stopped mid-sentence and looked at my mother's distraught face. She looked like a small child who just had her ice cream taken away. I had never seen an expression like that on my mother's face before.

"Tell you what. After we see Doctor Dreayer, I'll get out the picnic basket, and we'll make peanut butter sandwiches with bananas! How does that sound?" I was acting like a parent, who changes the subject and rambles on about anything in order to avoid a meltdown.

"Okay," my mother replied. Spinning on her heels, she walked out of the room.

"I'll be ready to go in ten minutes," she said, smiling happily, as she closed my door behind her.

Hmmm guess I won't be taking that bath after all, I said to myself.

• • •

I hadn't seen Doctor Dreayer since my father died. He seemed a lot older than he had even a couple of years ago. He still reminded me of Sigmund Freud, his signature beard now entirely gray. I wondered if he had ever shaved it off for any period of time in all these years. He was a kind, gentle soul and seemed to know what he was doing. The fact that he was still practicing, let alone still standing, was a miracle in my book. He had been my parents' physician for eons.

When I walked into his office the smells that permeated the room made me flash back to my youth. There was always the presence of alcohol mixed with an earthy undertone. The good Doctor was obviously a closeted pipe smoker. He had models of various body parts always at the ready. He loved to pick them up and show the insides of a heart or a lung to any willing patient.

My mother and I sat across from his desk, which was covered and strewn with papers and files. I hadn't a clue how he could find anything. He began flinging different papers aside and muttering to himself that he knew what he was looking for was "around here someplace!" When he found whatever he was looking for, he seemed astonished that he had.

"So . . . Olivia . . . and Sarah, of course," he said, nodding in my direction. "As you know from the last few tests, you have entered a new phase of dementia. The drug that we began you with seems to be helping." He busily scanned his notes, flipping pages, going back to previous ones, muttering to himself. He seemed to be dotty.

"Doctor," I interjected. "I was told that my mother has Alzheimer's . . . "

"Shhhh. For God's sake, don't use that word," my mother interrupted. "We had an agreement. Isn't that right doc? No use of that word."

Doctor Dreayer looked at me as if I'd just robbed a bank. "We had an agreement," he concurred.

"Well, I didn't know about it," I said. "I'm sorry." I felt like the girl in school who was the only one who didn't know that Andrew had kissed Emily in the girl's bathroom.

Dreayer scanned both our faces, assessing us, then said, "Olivia, would you mind if I had a word with Sarah? Alone?"

Without hesitation, my mother stood up and said she would go get some coffee.

"Wow. That was easy," I said, watching the door shut behind her. The doctor and I stared at one another for a while. My knee jumped up and down under his desk, totally impatient woman that I am. And then, I couldn't help myself, I asked "What's up doc?" He didn't laugh.

"You are aware of the Alzheimer diagnosis, but has your mother told you about her cancer?"

"Her what?" I asked even though I had heard him in the first place.

"She has lung cancer."

I sat there shocked, not knowing how to respond. "You're saying that my mother has cancer in addition to Alzheimer's?"

"Yes," he replied.

I was beginning to wonder just how many more surprises would hit me between the eyes on this trip. "How long?" I took a deep breath and shook in my shoes.

"If you're asking how long has she has known? A year. How long does she have? Hard to say." He paused, taking off his glasses. "Your mother has refused conventional treatments and actually has quite a sense of humor about it. Her response to it all was, "At least I have Alzheimer's, so I won't remember I have cancer." The doctor smiled.

I was surprised by her wit, but I didn't find it all that amusing. We sat in silence for a bit, then he cleared his throat.

"She asked me to talk to you at some point and to ask you to agree to the same request that your father made before he died."

Now my head was swirling and my heart racing. I was afraid to hear what he had to tell me.

Sensing I was totally out in the cold, the good Doc filled me in. "Your father had several prescriptions. Your mother was to help him when the time was right . . . "

I began to catch on at this point. Music started to play in my brain and bitter saliva began forming in my mouth. "Are you telling me that my mother helped with an assisted suicide? For my father?"

He looked at me squarely, and began straightening out his pipe collection in front of him. "We were never to discuss the outcome. I don't know what she administered if anything. Your father was in the final stages of congestive heart failure and wanted to go with some dignity. The weaker his heart became, the more difficulty he had with his breathing . . . " The doctor stopped for a moment. "It was to be between the two of them."

"And you were okay with that?" I got out of my chair. "You are a man of medicine, for Christ's sake. Not Jack Kevorkian!"

He nodded. "I am also their friend."

With that, I no longer felt my legs, the room spun around, and I was out like a light.

If you have to lose consciousness, the doctor's office is the place to do it. I highly recommend it. The response is quick and methodical. As I came to, Dr. Dreayer was bent over me with smelling salts under my nose. I think he may have slapped me.

"You okay, Sarah?"

My eyelids fluttered and I nodded. I knew that I hadn't hit my head. After almost forty odd years of this happening, I had become proficient at passing out safely.

"You are still fainting I see," he stated. "And you were singing . . . Barry Manilow . . . I think."

"Bobby Sherman," I replied, peeling myself off the floor. I assured him I had been checked from head to toe regarding my tendency to faint. I even had a defibrillator standing by at one point. What I finally learned is that I stop breathing when I am under stress. And we all know what happens then, don't we?

The doctor assisted me back into a chair. I continued where I had left off. "Okay, back to the discussion in progress. At what point did my mother think that maybe I would consider helping her with. . ." I couldn't even say it.

Doctor Dreayer lowered himself into his old oak swivel chair. He picked up his glasses, once more, and perched them on his nose. "I really am not allowed to discuss what it is either. Anything that a patient decides to do to help ease the final stages of an illness, I am all for, as a human being. As a physician, such a course of action cannot be something that I prescribe."

"How long have you known this family?"

"About thirty years."

"So you are aware what my mother has done to herself in the past?"

Doctor Dreayer nodded.

"So, here we are, years after my mother's multiple attempts at suicide, now she wants somebody to assist her?"

Doctor Dreayer cast his eyes to the floor.

I stood up abruptly. "Well, I'm not doing it! No fucking way. I saved her sorry ass far too many times as a child. She can't expect me to bloody kill her now myself! Don't you see the irony in this?"

"Look Sarah, I don't think that's the ultimate decision on her part. All I know is that when she first received her Alzheimer's diagnosis, she brought up the fact that she didn't want to be so far gone that she wouldn't know her family anymore. Months later when she learned about the cancer, she didn't want you or your brother to have to suffer along with her. That's the same way your father felt."

"I know you're just the messenger Doc, but the whole thing is insane." I turned toward the door and looked back. "How long before one, or both, illnesses kill her?"

"The cancer? Probably six months. She could live with Alzheimer's . . . for years."

I nodded. "I guess I'll be seeing you more on a regular basis then?"

Doctor Dreayer nodded as we said our good-byes and I walked into the waiting room. My mother was chatting with one of the nurses. I didn't even want to look at her.

"Come on Mother. Let's go," I said, brushing past her.

On the drive home, I knew she was aware of my anger, but she didn't say anything. All I could think of was getting back to the house and calling my brother, Henry, to see if he had heard anything about this craziness.

When we pulled into the driveway, Mother got out of the car announcing that she wanted to check on the garden. That probably meant Manuel, but whatever. She went one way, and I went the other. I knew my mother had Henry on speed dial, so I took the house phone from its cradle and dialed my brother's number. After going through all the machinations of secretaries and nurses to reach my brother, the Doctor finally picked up the line. "Sissy? That you?"

I didn't bother to say hello. I just launched into an account of everything that had gone on in my few days at the family homestead. "Mother may be losing the house. She is definitely losing her mind. Did you know that she has cancer, too? Did anyone ever tell you that dad had wanted her to assist him in death? And now she was asking me to do the same for her?"

Basically, my brother said "No. No. No. And no!" His voice was calm. He didn't seem surprised upon learning about all these disasters.

"Aren't you at all concerned about what I'm telling you?"

"Of course I am, Sarah. I guess I'm trying to process it all. Maybe after you calm down a little, we can go over everything one item at a time."

"Calm down!?" I yelled into the mouthpiece. "You have no idea what's going on here. Calm down, my ass! Don't be condescending, Henry. Maybe when you stop being the doctor man and start being the son- brother- man, we can talk." I hung up the phone on the one person who understood me better than anyone else in the world. I shot up the stairs, like a twelve-year-old, flew into my room, slammed my door, and threw myself weeping onto the horrible sofa bed.

I'm not sure when my brother was suddenly better at everything than me. In our early years, I was substantially better at everything. It frustrated the hell out of him, because I could throw a ball, bat a ball, bowl a ball, kick a ball, head a ball, so much better than he could. I could ride a bike, ride a horse, skateboard, roller skate and ice skate without ever falling. On the other hand, he always had skinned knees, cut lips, stitches in his chin and head while I occasionally suffered a bruise.

He was certainly better at showing his emotions than I was. He used to get so upset with me that he would fling himself to the ground and scream. He could also be the sweetest, most polite little boy in the world. Around the time Henry turned fifteen, everything changed. He must have caught up developmentally. He became a sports fanatic, and I couldn't keep up. Not that I really wanted to. He also became a brainiac. He read constantly about history, the human body and mind, space, you name it. He became our dad's pride and joy.

I was a senior at the time he came into his own and couldn't wait to go away to college. I was definitely proud of Henry, but he never knew it. The fact that our father paid so much attention to Henry only made me angrier with my father. After I figured out my father was having an affair, it was hard for me to forgive him much of anything!

Henry wasn't told about dad and Helen's affair until years later. I had to swear not to say anything or risk the wrath of the belt. I probably never would have known either, if I hadn't seen it for myself.

Around the time of my thirteenth birthday, my mother attempted to commit suicide for the third time. She was in the hospital again to have her stomach pumped. I wasn't sure if my birthday party would happen with her in the hospital again. On our visit the second day of her stay, Dad announced he had to go make a call from the pay phone and asked me to keep an eye on Henry and mother. I don't know what caused me to feel suspicious. Not long after he left the room, I told Henry to stay put, and I followed my father.

My dad didn't smoke around us, but we knew that he did. As I turned a corner in the hospital corridor, I smelled burning tobacco. I heard him speaking in hushed tones when I rounded another corner. I stopped in my tracks. A very tall, red- haired, quite beautiful woman was holding my dad in a very intimate way. He was murmuring softly to her in between his tears. She stroked the back of his head and repeatedly told him that it was okay. He held her tightly with one hand while he gripped his cigarette in the other. In an instant, I knew this woman was more than a friend. I realized that my relationship with my father was about to change.

He turned as if he sensed someone was watching, and his eyes caught mine. A variety of emotions flashed on his face: astonishment, fear, sadness, fight or flight, repulsion, guilt, redemption. As we stared at one another, I felt a gnawing sensation that began in my loins and traveled slowly up into my chest. I knew that tightness would soon be followed by the ringing in my ears and some stupid song, a sign that I might hit pavement. If I didn't get out of there, I was going to faint.

I took off running through doors and hospital hallways barely remembering where I was supposed to go. In complete panic, anger, fear, and frustration, I finally collapsed in a waiting room chair in a distant wing of the hospital and began to sob.

Crying for me has always been private. I didn't share the experience with many people. It was mine and mine alone. Not until I was an adult did I realize that I was probably just scared to cry . . . particularly in front of my mother. I had to be the strong one for her. If she saw me crying, she might feel guilty that she brought it on . . . and then what? Maybe she would succeed in killing herself. I could never take that chance. After a good ten minute cry in the waiting room I found a visitor's bathroom, washed my face, and emerged a bright and cheery thirteen-year-old. By the time I found my way back to my mother's hospital room, she and my brother were none the wiser.

I couldn't bear to look at my father for weeks after that. I understood his need to seek out female companionship, but I was still furious.

If he couldn't talk to my mother anymore, why couldn't he talk to me? Why did he need to bring in an outsider who had nothing to do with our family? I turned inward and barricaded myself in my room, listening to The White Album over and over and over.

• • •

On the first day of summer vacation, my father asked me to take a drive with him to the nursery. "We need to get your mother some flowers for her garden," he told me.

I agreed reluctantly.

On our way, my dad suggested we get a malt first. I think I'd have done just about anything for a chocolate malt. I knew somewhere down deep what he was doing was total manipulation, but I really didn't care. I was happy to be with my dad. We took up residence in the corner booth of the coffee shop. As soon we slid into the leather seats, my father said "I'm not seeing her anymore, Sarah."

I didn't know what to say.

"Did you hear me?"

I was thinking "Gee, Dad, that's terrific! What a shame Dad. Did you love her? Was she better than Mom? Would you still be with her if I hadn't caught you?" What was I, a thirteen-year-old kid, supposed to do with this information? I mean really! I did manage to say, "What's her name?"

"Her name is Helen," my father answered.

After that we sat sipping our malts in total silence. I was relieved that he didn't want to go on. I was not interested in a discussion about another woman in my dad's life.

At the nursery we picked out a variety of colorful, flowering plants for Mom's garden and piled them into the back of the Lincoln Continental. The wondrous smells of new plants, roses, hydrangeas, jasmine, softened the tense air as we drove home. My father hummed.

My mother was surprised, and thrilled with our selection. We rarely saw her thrilled by anything, so it felt good.

A couple of weeks later, I decided to drop by the library where my father gave lectures during the summer. I slipped into the University Hall just in time to see my dad and Helen having a tete-a-tete. Neither of them saw me. It didn't bother me this time. Maybe I was numb. Maybe I never really believed my dad in the first place. Maybe I was more understanding than I really knew. I never spoke about Helen to him again.

Years later, I learned that Helen moved away and eventually got married. My dad spent more time around the house, sometimes even helping mom tend to her garden. It was nice to have him there.

• • •

As I came to the end of my sobbing jag, I lifted my head from the sofa bed. Looking around again at what had been my father's sanctuary, I truly missed him.

A faint knock at the door interrupted my memories.

"Come in," I called out. My mother was at the door wearing a wide brimmed hat and carrying a picnic basket in her hand. Neither of us spoke. A broad smile spread across my face.

The pond near our house was always full of ducks. It was a short walk from where we lived. When I was little, I would save bread crusts and stale bread for them. I enjoyed feeding the greedy birds. It actually taught me patience. When I was old enough to go to the pond on my own, I would sometimes have to wait, with my treats, for them to notice me if they happened to be the other side of the water. The best part was when all the new hatchlings would swim furiously behind their parents and gobble up my bread in record time. I learned that ducks, geese, and swans are monogamous. Once mated, that's it. That knowledge made it impossible for me to consume these birds, for fear I was eating a life partner and its mate would forever live alone.

Years later I wondered why my father couldn't be like the mallards I was feeding.

When we arrived at the pond, my mother set down one of her heavy blankets on the damp grass. At four in the afternoon, it was cold, and the sky threatened rain again. I tried to be happy and enjoy this time with my mother. I plonked myself down hard onto the blanket, making a groaning sound on the way down. Another reminder that I wasn't getting any younger.

"Are you okay? You mentioned wanting to have a picnic earlier didn't you?" my mother asked, worried.

"I'm fine, Mother. And yes, I did mention it . . . this is lovely." I wasn't as furious with her as I had been earlier. Here we were alone on the pond about to eat peanut butter and jelly sandwiches. The ducks were upon us in no time and proceeded to eat most of my sandwich. My mother and I giggled.

"I'm sorry I didn't tell you," my mother began. "That I have cancer, I mean." She turned her face away.

"Well," I paused, "I can only say that I wished you had. Now that I do know we'll figure it out!"

"There isn't anything to figure out, Sarah. I'm going to die . . . and I hope it will be before my mind completely gives out!"

"Don't, Mom . . . please."

"Sarah, it's a fact. I probably don't have long. I want to tell you that I am thankful you are here, and I wish we could have done this a long time ago."

I couldn't believe what I was hearing. Was this really my mother? Were we actually having a moment? All I knew was that I liked whatever was happening.

I guess the lesson was for me to appreciate whatever time I had with my mother and not to analyze it too much. We sat for a while, not talking. Taking in the sights, the smells, the experience. Clouds darkened the horizon, and ducks puffed themselves up in preparation for the pending rain. People on the bike path peddled faster as small drops of rain fell.

"Guess we should head back, Mother," I said as I not so gracefully got up from the blanket.

Looking up at me, she nodded. I helped her get to her feet. As we stood facing one another, she smiled and said, "Thank you for a lovely picnic." She picked up the basket and began slowly to walk away. I watched as she walked a little ahead and realized how very frail she was, her body smaller that I remembered. I folded the blanket and soon caught up to her. Walking home as the rain got heavier, we tried to cover ourselves with one of the blankets.

Manuel had built a roaring fire in the living room. His face lit up when Mother walked in. I took the picnic basket from her as she reached for Manuel. They kissed lightly on the cheek.

"*Ola mija*," he cooed.

"*Ola mijo*," she responded.

Leaving them, I took myself into the kitchen and set down the basket. I noticed my cell phone blinking on the counter, indicating I had a message. I couldn't believe I had forgotten it. I was never without my cell phone. I had obviously been more pre-occupied with my mother's health news than I realized. It was a text from Henry. "Sorry Sis. Didn't mean to sound unconcerned. Let's talk. Still planning 2 b there Thxgvg. xxoo."

"Thanksgiving!!! Shit!" I said aloud. I continued to forget the Holiday was around the corner. I suppose I was expected to plan it all. By myself. As usual. I had begun to resent it. Why me? Why couldn't I be the one without the responsibilities for once? I would have to ponder this question at a later date, because I knew this holiday would fall on my shoulders. But damn if I was going to do Christmas!

I had to talk to Mother to see if any thought regarding this holiday had entered her head. I had no idea what were my kids planning or if Henry would bring his whole clan. Was I expected to invite other people?

I walked out of the kitchen to find Manuel holding onto my mother for dear life. She looked like an animal paralyzed in head lights. I asked Manuel what was going on.

"She says the water is too deep in front of her. She thinks the floor is water and she cannot cross."

"We will sink! We can't go this way," my mother protested. In less than twenty minutes, my mother had gone from a fairly normal state to the delusional woman in front of me, now a woman slowly losing her mind. My heart sank. Manuel scooped her up into his arms, and they crossed the imaginary water together. I watched him carry her up the stairs, gently whispering to her that all was well.

I stood for a moment reflecting when a loud crack of thunder made me jump. Simultaneously the doorbell rang. Shivers ran down my spine. When I opened the front door, and saw a shadow standing in the dimly lit front porch fumbling with something, I wondered if we were about to be robbed. There was a flash of lightning and another burst of thunder. I realized the figure was closing an umbrella. Like a scene from "*The Exorcist,*" the eerie figure turned to face me. I recognized the broad toothy smile almost immediately. It was Marie's and Terry's father, Robert.

"Sarah, my dear. How long it has been?"

I was speechless as I stared at a man I knew to be at least seventy-five years old, looking handsome and spry. "Mr. Beckett. What a surprise!" I invited him in.

He dropped his umbrella at the door and shook himself off like a giant poodle.

"I have news!" We walked into the toasty living room. "Terry told me you were here and that he had spoken to you regarding your mother and this house." He sat in the wingback as I landed on the couch.

"Yes, I hadn't heard any of this until Terry told me." I offered Robert a drink, which he declined.

"My firm received an anonymous donation a few days ago to cover whatever was owed on this house in full."

I tried to process what I was hearing. "An anonymous donor?" I repeated what he had said "How can that be? Who else knew that she owed money? I mean, I only just found out myself?"

"Well, I suppose your mother might have casually mentioned it to someone, or maybe someone saw papers that have been filed." Robert answered. "Your mother has made many friends over the years."

I sat in disbelief. It occurred to me to buy off the loan myself when Terry told me all of this, but in just a few days someone has come forward. Who has 100,000 dollars to give to my mother? And why? Someone who wants to remain anonymous. The entire scenario was surreal. Not that I minded. I mean, it gave me one less thing to worry about. I was more convinced than ever that this family had more skeletons in the closet than most other families.

"Now I have to ask another important question." He opened his briefcase. "Is your mother still of sound mind?"

"Other than the fact that she just thought our hallway was Lake Michigan . . . she's just swell!"

Robert glanced down.

"I didn't mean to make light of it," I apologized. "I am just beginning to learn about all this myself. Sometimes she seems as normal as can be. Then in an instant she doesn't know what a set of keys is used for!"

"Well, we need to discuss power of attorney and who should be in charge when and if she is unable to make normal decisions." He handed me some papers and suggested I look them over and have my mother read them as well. "If she understands what she is reading, have her sign the papers and get them back to me. As soon as you can approach the subject regarding power of attorney, give me a call, and I will have Terry draw up those papers as well."

I nodded that I understood.

As Robert got up, he said he had wanted to give me the news personally because he would be going to visit Marie and her family for Thanksgiving. I thanked him for coming and we walked together to the door. Robert grabbed his umbrella. The rain had subsided. We shook one another's hands before Robert stepped outside.

"Thank you so much, Mr. Beckett. I really appreciate your taking the time."

"Quite alright, Sarah. Our families have been through a lot over the years. It's the least I could do." He smiled, turned, and walked down the front steps. "By the way," he said, turning back, "It's Robert. Please call me Robert."

I nodded and smiled and remembered to ask him to send Marie my love when he saw her.

"Of course I will."

I watched and waited until his car pulled out of our driveway. I turned off all the lights before taking myself upstairs. Walking past my mother's closed door, I wondered what was going on behind it with Manuel. Actually, I don't think I really wanted to know. Who was this Manuel, really? Did he know that my mother was in debt? It occurred to me that I should see if Mother had a will. Does he think he may get something from her when she dies? After all he lives in a trailer in her back yard!

Once in my room, I retrieved the letter box from under my bed and read more of the letters. One by one, I pulled letters out and read them. Some were dated as far back as 1945, which would have made my mother about seventeen. The letters seem to have stopped around the late eighties. The letters in my mother's handwriting were addressed to "Father Manuel Garcia" and sent to the same church in Mexico. All the love letters were sent to a post office box here in Marin.

November, 16, 1946

I am writing this to you with dictionary in hand. It is one year since you are gone. I do not believe my heart will heal forever. I am now having taken my vows. I pray to God that my love can only be for Him. When your face is in front of me in my dreams, I must ask God to make you go from my head. I love my people and the church, and I will do my best for them. Yours Manuel

One letter, after another. Two tormented lovers. Is this the same Manuel in my Mom's bedroom? If the man in these letters was a man of God, a priest, what had he and my mother hope to do? The Manuel I was reading about in the letters obviously had a deep faith. My mother had lost all her faith a long time ago.

We were not brought up overly religious. My parents did go to church, and the three of us kids attended Sunday school. I tried hard to be a believer at an early age. The older I got, the more I envied people with deep-rooted beliefs. I was told early on that I had too many questions about the Bible, faith, and religion in general. In my mind, religion was the reason for most of the world's war. As a child, I asked my teachers about that fact. They were continually frustrated and annoyed with me, so I stopped asking.

I had two friends in high school, of different faiths. Debbie was a Christian Scientist and, Rachel, a Jew. I tried to wrap my head around certain things they had told me about their beliefs. Some of it intrigued me.

Debbie, my Christian Science friend, came to visit me one day after realizing I had been out of school for several days. I had had a strep throat. Debbie asked me what it was I was trying to avoid? What did I not want to discuss? She told me she believed that I had created this illness to avoid something else. She went on to explain that if my body created sickness, my body could get rid of it, too. She claimed I didn't need medicine. What she said made sense to me.

One day, a few months later, a bunch of us were out riding our bikes. A car hit Debbie's bike, sending her flying into the gravel. Her body was badly scraped, and her knee had completely split open. We stayed with her until her father came. Debbie tried so hard to be strong and not let the pain get to her. There was a lot of blood and bone was exposed. The man who had hit her kept insisting she should get to a hospital. When the police showed up, they wanted to call an ambulance. Debbie said that she had to wait for her father and that he would take care of it all. When her dad arrived, he thanked everyone and proceeded to pile Debbie into the back of their car. He took her home where she was put on the couch and fed ice cream sundaes because she was so "brave." It took weeks for her leg to heal, and she walked with a limp from then on.

I heard, years later that her first child had died. She had been stricken with a horrible cancer and died a painful death, because the family wouldn't allow any form of medication for her. That faith lost points with me.

Rachel, my Jewish friend, had a fabulous family. I went to Temple with them occasionally and even celebrated Chanukah with them a few times. Judaism always seemed like a civilized religion to me. I loved the idea of Yom Kippur, the day of atonement, and wondered why everyone couldn't have a day like that to reflect, to thank God for his blessings and forgiveness without consequence in a single day.

While Rachel and I were doing homework one night I asked her if she believed in miracles.

"Of course I believe in miracles," she replied.

"Then why doesn't your faith believe that Christ was conceived immaculately?" I asked.

"Oh, come on, Sarah . . . do you really believe that?" She snorted.

"I don't know what I believe, that's why I'm asking," I responded. Then I put it to her. "If you believe in the Old Testament, do you really believe Moses parted the Red Sea? Or that Noah was three hundred years old when he built the Arc?"

We sat in silence for a really long time. And the next day, our friendship ended.

I wanted to have faith. I still do. The people I knew who had a deep connection to their faith always seemed happier. I tried. Really hard! After all, when you stare at the face of a newborn child, it's easy to believe in God. But when a baby is brutally murdered in the Congo, where is the God I am supposed to believe in then?

We had been a fairly normal, loving family before Rachel died. It's hard to remember now. Our dad spent more time at home. We went out more as a family. My parents were social, and our house was the entertainment hub. My mother had dinner parties several times a month. I remember lying in my bedroom and hearing laughter and clinking glasses from downstairs. We always had a roaring fire to set the mood, even in the summertime. Our house was a home, a happy home. All that changed when Rachel died. When her light went out it was as if she took all luminosity with her. My own eight-year-old world became dark and cold. I retreated into myself and discovered that I like looking at things differently. I loved to hang upside down for long periods of time, imagining I could walk on the ceiling or swing from the chandelier or hang from tree branches and float on the clouds. Everything looked better upside down. I would wait until the blood rushed to my head, and I would hear the now familiar warning sound of my heart pounding, then I would right myself. I always stopped before I fainted. I pushed it to the limit. I actually liked whatever that feeling was.

Back then I tried to speak to God, mostly because I didn't feel I could talk to anyone else. It became clear that what I asked him for wasn't going to happen. Rachel didn't come back, my mother still disappeared into her world of grief, and my father continued to spend more and more time away from home. I became as silent as God was with me.

I set down the box of letters and wondered if my mother had been searching too.

Oh my God! It hit me then. This was indeed the same Manuel! He isn't really a gardener. I knew that from the start. Maybe the two of them shared a spiritual connection in the early days too, both of them searching. Both of them vulnerable in their teens. If I was reading about the same person who was shacked up with my mother right now, I couldn't have written a better story! But I was still not completely sure what was between them.

The only thing I was certain about was that I needed a midnight snack. I figured Manuel and my mother were tucked away together behind her closed door. In the kitchen I noticed my cell phone was blinking. I had two text messages. The first was from Dwight. I didn't remember giving him my cell number. It read: "Hey, sexy, thinkin' bout you hard. Sending you a pic." The next text which was a multimedia text also from Dwight. It was a photo of his very hard penis! Talk about a whole new world of endless possibilities.

I wasn't sure how to return the text. Should I snap a photo of my genitalia and tell him it was nice to hear from him? Or maybe I should just drive over to his place and make sure he's alright. He might need some help! I picked up the phone and pressed reply. I typed in: NICE. Very original. I saved the photo for later. Maybe I could use this new technology in another book. I laughed at the thought.

I looked out into the garden at Manuel's spaceship. My curiosity spurred me into action. It would be a good time to investigate this Manuel.

I knocked on the trailer door. No one answered. I knocked again a little louder this time. Still, there was no answer. I opened the door and peeked in. The place was immaculate. Not a dust bunny anywhere. The bed was even made with hospital corners. The spot where the built in sofa would normally be located in an airstream had been replaced by a full on altar. A ceramic Virgin Mary stood on a marble countertop, her hands open toward the heavens. A rosary lay at her feet and an open prayer book next to the rosary. When I scanned the small space, I was thrown by the sheer number of photographs that lined the walls. Almost all of the shots were of my mother at various stages of her life, from around eighteen to the present day. She looked beautiful in each shot, and she wore a brilliant, happy smile in all of them. I was unaccustomed to that smile. Okay, this tour now convinced me that this is the same Manuel as the Father Manuel of my mother's correspondence. I stood a while longer trying to take it all in. I backed slowly from the doorway and into the damp night. I couldn't get over the sight of my mother's smiling face in all the photographs, so loving, content, so happy. An acute pang of envy rose inside me at the idea that someone other than her family had known that side of her.

As I made my way back to the house, I saw the curtain of my mother's room open. She looked down at me as we stared at one another. She must have seen me leaving Manuel's trailer and I didn't know how she would react. She raised her hand and waved at me before she disappeared behind the curtain.

"Oh, my God, we so have to talk," I muttered as I walked back into the kitchen. I picked up my phone, remembering my little photo treat from Dwight and wondered how I should respond.

Her breath struggled to keep up with the pounding of her feet on the hard sand, for she stuck close to the shore line. It was low tide, and the light from the brilliant full moon cascaded onto the distant calm waters. She could taste the salt on her cheeks, from her tears, not the ocean. Her heart beat so hard she thought it might explode from her chest. All she could do was run, run away, run fast, run hard. It didn't matter where. She just had to get away. Away from her past, away from all of them, away from him and most of all away from herself.

The sound of thunderous steps pounded into the sand behind her. She didn't look back for fear the entire town was chasing her. She had made a spectacle of herself at the restaurant. Thinking that Paul had betrayed her with another woman, she had smashed her glass to the floor and screamed as she ran out the doors onto the beach. She knew people came out after her, calling her name in the night. She felt like Joan of Arc before her capture. As hard and fast as she ran, the steps behind her got closer, until she heard deep, heavy breathing, like a dragon bearing down on her. She felt the hot, fiery breath at the base of her neck. She turned around just as the giant stallion caught up to her.

Before she knew it, she was swept up with tremendous force and placed atop the powerful, bellowing beast. The man behind her was Paul Rodriguez.

"You cannot leave me," the sexy Spaniard breathed into her ear. Pulling back the reins of his horse, he forced her to look at him. She stared at him through her tears, and he gently kissed them away.

"I love you," he declared in a seductive voice. "I will take care of you and love you. We shall be forever one . . . together."

He jumped off the horse and stared up at her. He extended his hand toward her, and she took it. Back on the sand, she faced her biggest challenge. Though the man of her dreams stood before her, she could never allow love into her life. She had always resisted hoping for true happiness. She never felt she deserved it. But here was her white knight, someone who had eyes for her alone . . .

The waves lapped at their feet, the gentle wind kissed their skin. He took her face in his hands and parted her lips with his tongue. Her knees went weak. A longing grew between

*her legs as she pressed her body into his.
Falling into each other, they collapsed onto
the sand. They breathed as one. Her heart beat
in her ears, matching the rhythm of the tide.
When Paul ripped off his shirt, she tasted the
salt on his skin. He couldn't wait any longer.
He reached under her damp skirt to pull away
her panties. He was inside her before she knew
it. She moaned, as loud as the roar of the
waves. In that moment, they created a symphony
all their own. They lay together watching
the beginnings of the sun peeking over the
horizon in the warm, tequila sunrise night.*

THE END

I closed the laptop and thanked God I had finally finished the book from hell. Exhausted, I had to have a look at Dwight on my phone. I stared at his impressive cock and decided the photo deserved a more appropriate response. I was not up to speed with modern technology. I wasn't that great with a regular camera either, let alone the one that existed on my cell phone, but I thought I'd give it a whirl. If nothing else I could chalk it up to research. I could call my next book *Textual Healing.*

I stripped, leaving on my fuchsia panties. I looked around the room for inspiration as to what to do next. Nothing original came to mind, so I positioned myself on the sofa bed in what I thought a sexy position without being too pornographic. I held my cell phone at arm's length above me, trying to capture the full effect without being close enough to show any flaws. I closed my eyes, feigning tranquil bliss and pushed the little button. Click. I was excited to view my masterpiece. I had a look only to discover I had taken a perfectly lovely photo of the ceiling.

I decided to try again. Maybe I should touch myself, be more provocative. I slipped my left hand into my bra cupping my breast and held the camera in my right hand. Okay. I set up the shot, then fumbled around trying to locate the button with my left hand. I needed two hands! Click. The phone leapt out of my hands like a bar of wet soap. It skidded across the hardwood floor. I crawled around on my hands and knees in my sexy underwear groping for the phone. I finally located it under the Lazy- boy recliner.

Okay. One more time. I took the shot standing up. I could hold the phone in both hands stretched out in front of me. I stuck the typical Marilyn Monroe pose with one leg crossed in front of the other and gave a sexy, come hither smile . . . Click. I was sure I had it this time. And I did. The only problem was the shot only captured my breasts. I was a torso totally headless and legless. I gave up and wrote the message "this is 4 u" and pushed send.

I waited and waited. Maybe it was too late. He had texted me his penis more than an hour earlier. He's probably long gone. I went to the bathroom to do my nighttime ritual. Then I heard the little beep beep of my phone. What a lovely sound. I was giddy when I saw it was from Dwight. His message read, "Really hot, Sarah!!!"

Whoa, this was fun. I was actually turned on that he was turned on by my photo. I texted back "Now it's ur turn!!" And I pushed send.

Again, I waited. And waited a lot longer this time. I clicked on the television and watched a few minutes of the depressing news. I clicked it off and found myself staring at the phone, willing it to beep. My heart raced when it finally did. I couldn't wait to see how he had responded. I opened the message, and there was Dwight's cock in what could only be described as a cum shot. There his magnificent penis rested, on top of his waxed stomach with the gift of life next to it. His message read, "THANX . . . That was great."

I sat bewildered staring at the phone, not sure what my next move should be. I texted back the only thing I could think of . . . "Ur Welcome."

Maybe this is how lovers communicate these days. It did feel incredibly intimate. But I did miss the moaning and groaning that happens when you're at least in the same room with your lover. I was wiped out even though I hadn't had an orgasm. My co-dependent self was happy that someone did. I put my hair up on top of my head, smeared on an evening face masque and slipped into my flannel pj's. How un-sexy could I be? I climbed into my bed, decided to delete the sexy texts, just in case. Wouldn't you know it . . . ? I had the best night's sleep in a really long time.

As the light squeezed through the tiny slats of my blinds the next morning, I could hear Manuel and my mother talking in the driveway. I peered out the window and saw mother in the new staple of her wardrobe, another florescent jogging suit. She looked like a Muppet. Manuel was next to her, holding a stopwatch.

"Oh, Lord, she's gonna race herself to death," I thought. I threw on my sweats and raced downstairs. I opened the front door just as Manuel yelled "GO!" My mother took off.

More than upset by what I had just seen, I blurted out, "What are you doing Manuel? She can't race!"

"No, no, Miss Sarah it's not that. She doesn't run . . . not really. Just in her head."

"What do you mean she doesn't run? She jogs all the time! And the idea of her trying to pick up speed . . . !"

"She goes to the road and sits on the bench at the end of the road," he explained.

"She doesn't jog?" I thought maybe I hadn't heard correctly.

"No, Miss Sarah, she doesn't do much of anything she says anymore. Just in her mind."

"Wow . . . " I shook my head. "I'm sorry, Manuel. I shouldn't have yelled at you."

"It's okay, Miss Sarah. I understand."

I had to question all the other things I assumed my mother was doing. I had to ask. "Manuel . . . You and my mother? . . . Do you have intimate relations?"

"Oh my . . . I mean we are both older now . . . that was all a very long time ago," he responded, looking at his feet.

"So, those letters you gave me to read? Are you the Father Manuel my mother was writing to?"

"Yes, Miss Sarah. I have loved Miss Olivia since the day I saw her. We were like children, fifteen and sixteen, but we shared a big love."

"Oh, Manuel . . . I don't know what to say. We have to talk about all of this. I need to understand what went on between the two of you, and I know I won't get it out of my mother."

Manuel nodded. "I think we should speak, too."

I felt tears threatening behind my eyes. "How long does she sit on the bench Manuel?"

He looked at his watch. "Sometimes a few minutes, sometimes an hour," he shrugged.

I told him I wanted to go to her, and he understood.

I rounded the corner from our driveway and, sure enough, there was Mother at the end of the cul de sac, sitting alone on the old, wooden bench. I approached quietly and sat.

She was staring straight out in front of her. "If you look very closely, you can see Rachel in the tree," she said, pointing to an old oak. "When I come here, she visits me."

I sat staring at the same tree almost hopeful, but I could only see the familiar oak tree I climbed as a kid. We sat in silence. I gazed at the neighborhood and the different types of trees. The old oak now resembled the one in *The Giving Tree*. Her branches hung much lower than I remembered, but her stature was still proud. There had been a sweet blue and white ranch style home, across the street, where a woman bred Yorkshire Terriers. She invited us to visit any time a new litter of puppies were born. They were so tiny. I loved their sweet puppy milk breath. Where the sweet house once stood was a much too large Spanish style home. Most of the other homes in the neighborhood had stayed the same, which was reassuring somehow.

"I think Rachel has been calling me more lately," my mother explained.

"Do you ever see Dad?" I asked.

"Who?"

"My father. Your husband?"

"He was a teacher, right? A handsome teacher . . . yes, I remember." Her voice trailed off. "He doesn't visit anymore. He broke my heart!"

Tears came rolling down my face at record speed. I wanted to tell my mother all that I had felt. Tell her how my heart had also been broken. Not only did I lose Rachel, but I lost who my mother had been before my sister's death. And now I was losing her again. I didn't say a word.

My mother began to cough, and I heard a slight rattle deep in her chest.

"I think we should go, Mom," I suggested, using the back of my sleeve to wipe my face.

"Ah, yes," she said and stood. "Burt Lancaster is on at three. *Elmer Gantry* I think. I love that Burt Lancaster." She turned to face me. "Oh, Sarah. Hello. When did you get here?"

"Just now, Mom. Just now." I looped my arm through hers and walked slowly back to the house. Manuel was standing in the exact spot waiting for our return.

Realizing that every moment, every breath, must be savored to the fullest, I decided to throw the best Thanksgiving this family had ever seen. Or at least try.

Chapter Seven

Karmic Relief

The next couple of days were hectic. E-mails flew back and forth between various family members. My agent had invited herself to the holiday as well. Lily was coming with a new boyfriend, and Phoebe finally shared her deep secret. To my great relief she had decided to go to culinary school to become a chef. To my even greater relief she announced that she wanted to do most of the cooking. Henry would be coming alone. My brother's wife, Lucy, is pregnant again and throwing up 24/7.

Manuel helped me locate the fine china my mother had put away years ago and the leaves to expand the cherry wood dining table. After my parents made the decision not to entertain any longer, everything had been packed up and stored somewhere in the basement. The leaves had actually retained a rich, dark color, while the rest of the table was at least two shades lighter. A table cloth could take care of that. Mother seemed delighted that the house would be filled with people, but she still asked Manuel what Thanksgiving was.

I took myself into town in search of some festive decorations. As I was browsing the shelves of the local gift store, I heard a low voice call my name. It was Robert Beckett. "Mister Bec . . . I mean Robert.

I thought you would be with Marie and her family by now." A flash in his eyes and a grimace indicated something wasn't right.

"Is everything okay? Is Marie alright?"

"I s'pose she is," he responded with sadness in his voice. "She is here with me. Just arrived. She left her husband!"

He was evidently upset by the news, and I worried that my relief would show through.

I did the only thing I thought appropriate. I invited Robert and Marie to join us for Thanksgiving. I counted in my head, myself, Mother, Manuel, Lily, Phoebe, Lily's boyfriend, my crazy agent Sybil, Henry, Marie, and Robert. That put the count at ten people now. The more the merrier. I was excited at the prospect of everyone being together to celebrate a holiday, rather than a sad event. I bought a perfect table cloth in a warm pumpkin color and matching napkins. I found tapered candles with maple leaves pressed into the wax to put in Grandma's silver candelabras. Martha Stewart would have been proud.

When I returned home, I saw that I had a couple of e-mails. One was from Phoebe with the menu she planned to prepare: A creamy butternut squash soup or pureed chestnut soup, a mixed green salad with a Meyer lemon vinaigrette, followed by a traditional roasted turkey, roasted root vegetables, and vanilla bean mashed potatoes. Dessert would consist of a mixed berry crumble, pumpkin pie, and pear tart.

I was impressed, especially since I wasn't aware that she even knew how to crack an egg! In the P.S she asked if I could do all the shopping and promised another e-mail with the shopping list. I was pleased that Phoebe finally was trying to make a go out of being responsible instead of getting another tattoo or piercing. Our relationship has been better lately. I think she has forgiven me for leaving her father, even though he was the one who screwed everything up.

Hunger pangs drove me toward the kitchen. My cell phone rang. I was hoping it was Dwight. The phone episodes the previous nights, had left me feeling vulnerable and wanting more at the same time. As I looked at the caller ID, I saw Marie was calling.

"Hey, Sarah . . . it's me," she said in a small voice. I immediately heard the pain.

"Hi, Marie. Yeah, I saw it was you! How are you?"

"I'm hangin', you know? Actually I'm pretty good . . . " She paused. "I heard you saw my dad and you invited us for Thanksgiving. That's really sweet of you, Sarah."

"I know," I said, laughing.

"Well, I was hoping to see you before all of that so we can sit and talk. Tell you what's going on."

"Of course. I thought the same thing."

"Great! How's tonight at seven at Stone Manor? I made a reservation."

What was it with her family and that restaurant? I wanted to see Marie. And even better, it was Monday. Dwight would probably be there working, too. I love the "two birds with one stone" thing. I accepted maybe a little too enthusiastically.

Manuel was cooking something wonderful when I stepped into the kitchen that evening. My mother was puttering around him trying to look efficient. Turning, she noticed me and asked where I was going. I was wearing a herringbone pencil skirt, a crisp white poplin shirt, bare legs, and a pair of high heels that I probably shouldn't wear anymore, but my legs look pretty damn good in them. "I'm meeting Marie for dinner, Mom," I replied.

"Who's Marie?" she asked.

Instead of getting into it, I answered, "She's just a friend, Ma."

"There will be a lot of food later, Miss Sarah, if you are hungry," Manuel said. "Chile con carne, tamales . . . "

"Smells amazing, Manuel. Next time?" I turned to leave. I was running a few minutes late. Since Marie was chronically late, I was hoping I'd have a moment alone with Dwight.

When I got to the restaurant, Marie predictably wasn't there yet. My heart was skipping as I anticipated seeing Dwight. I couldn't believe

I had feelings for a waiter so much younger than I. As I rounded the corner and stepped into the restaurant, I spotted him at a table. He saw me and flashed his huge, toothy smile, and my face instantly registered a wonderful shade of plum. Why would having wild sex with this man, and a texting escapade, embarrass me?

The hostess recognized me and asked if I wanted a table. When I told her I was meeting Marie, she gushed, "Oh, Miss Beckett, yes. We have her favorite table ready." She ushered me to a table in a cozy nook by the fireplace. I was thanking her just as Marie bounded in. She always walked with confidence. I hadn't seen her in a few years and she looked stunning. Her hair had been highlighted and cut in a trendy shag. She had either been sitting in the sun on some tropical island or visiting a tanning booth somewhere, because her skin was a golden brown. I jumped to my feet, and the two of us hugged one another for a long time. I could tell that she was smelling my hair, breathing me in. We sat down across from one another. Grinning.

At that point, Dwight approached our table. "Well, Sarah . . . it's been way too long." He smiled.

Of course I blushed again. Marie's expression made it clear she had immediately caught on that something was up between us. As a quick diversion, I ordered a bottle of Pinot Noir, a favorite of ours. Dwight winked at me before he walked away.

Marie eyed Dwight's rear. "Probably gay, right?"

"Actually, no," I defended my waiter.

Marie raised her eyebrows. "You seem awfully confident about that, Sarah. Anything you want to tell me?"

I brushed it off and told her that we were here to talk about her, not me. She looked at me for the longest time until I couldn't stand it anymore. "Marie? What the fuck?" I blurted. "Why didn't you call me or something? Let me know what's going on?"

She shook her head. "It happened very quickly."

"Is David's issue getting worse?" I asked.

"No. It has nothing to do with David really. It had to do with Lifetime."

"Okay," I said in disbelief. "Lifetime, as in movie channel?" I tried not to smile or giggle.

She sat back in her chair, obviously trying to frame her response.

"Look, I love those movies. Don't get me wrong, Marie, but what are you talkin' bout girl?"

Dwight returned with the wine. Marie didn't take her eyes off him as he opened the bottle and poured a taster in my glass and waited for me to taste it. I swirled the wine around in the bottom of my glass, then smelled its bouquet. As I went in for the first sip, I somehow missed my mouth completely and splattered my white shirt with the red wine. Instantly, Dwight had my napkin in my water and was trying to blot my left breast dry. The two of us fumbled for the napkin and a lot of "Oh dear's" "God, how clumsy" "I'll get soda water" were exchanged between us while Marie sat looking on. I finally wrestled the napkin from Dwight and said it wasn't a big deal and would take care of it later. He finished pouring our wine, and touched my hand, and walked away.

"Come on, Sarah, what's up with you and waiter man?"

"Oh no you don't. Don't try to change the subject on me. If you tell me about your cable distraction, then maybe I'll tell you about my waiter man."

Marie drew in a deep breath and stretched like a feline. I could see that she wasn't wearing a bra. Her breasts still had a youthful lift. She always had great breasts. I remembered that she never breast fed her babies.

"About a month ago," she began, "I was watching this film, 'The Secret Lives of Housewives.' The kids were with our new nanny, Rebecca, whom we had hired six months prior, a pretty eighteen-year-old from Scotland. I hadn't been feeling very sexual toward David for a long time. I knew it wasn't uncommon for women to lose some of their sex drive after children, so I didn't give it a second thought."

"You don't think it may have been something to do with his propensity toward your underwear?" I interrupted.

"No . . . it really didn't. In fact, I began to find it a little endearing. It was more than that. I joined a book club a few months ago and became friends with a woman. I found I could talk to her about everything." She stopped to sip her wine, and I took a big swig of mine.

"So that's a good thing. You made a friend, but what does this have to do with some movie?"

"It was based on a true story about these married women in a small town, who were saying the same things that I had been feeling . . . " She stopped again and looked away.

"Marie? Why is this so hard?" I asked. "We have been friends our whole lives."

"Sarah . . . I'm gay!" She blurted out.

Music swelled in my head and "At the Copa Cabana" began.

"Sarah?? Snap out of it!" Marie, all too familiar with my tendency to faint, tried to get my attention. Marie had her glass of water in hand, ready to toss it in my face if needed. She knew that sometimes prevented me from face planting. Just as I was focusing, my friend Dwight brought out an amuse bouche from the chef.

One look at my face, Dwight asked, "Is everything okay?"

"Oh yes, Dwight! Thank you for asking!" I said in a ladylike voice. "I just need a shot of tequila if you wouldn't mind!" I popped the chef's treat in my mouth without even asking what it was. The blood rushed back to my head.

"I thought you'd understand, Sarah . . . out of everyone!" Marie began to cry.

"Hey, hey, wait a minute, Marie. It's not that I don't understand what you just told me, I just don't get why you didn't open up to me about this before. Jesus, Marie, you and I delved into that for a while. Any time I brought it up with you, you acted as if it never happened. I'm a little hurt that you didn't feel you could talk to me." I reached into my purse and grabbed a tissue and handed it to her. She blew her nose long and hard.

"I'm talking to you now, Sarah!" Tears were still running down her face. "I didn't totally understand what was happening. I'd been with several women over the years. I think I got married to avoid the issue."

"Wait a minute!" I stopped her. "Several women? I never knew any of this!" I suddenly felt very territorial. "I thought I was the only . . . " I sounded like a five-year-old.

Marie just shook her head.

"You guys ready to order?" Dwight was back.

"No!" we said simultaneously, staring at him.

"I mean, not yet . . . " I tried to sound a little less hostile. He set my tequila down and gave me a puppy dog look before he left. I downed the shot immediately. It was like fire in my throat and burned all the way down to my belly. It was perfect.

"Marie, why don't you order? And I'll have the same. I'm going to the ladies room. Excuse me," I said, and pushed back my chair. I had to take a breather. I needed to wrap my head around what Marie was telling me, maybe deal with the stain on my shirt, and apologize to sweet, sexy Dwight for snapping at him. As I entered the hallway, Dwight was on my heels. He caught my arm.

"Dwight, I'm so sorry for snapping at you . . . " I had barely gotten the words out of my mouth before he pushed open the door to the handicap restroom and shoved me inside. He locked the door behind us. His long fingers were all over me as we kissed and stumbled and banged into the walls. Before I knew it, my pencil skirt was pushed up around my waist and Dwight's trousers were down around his ankles. He spun me around to face the wall and yanked down my panties. He thrust himself inside me from behind. I heard a squeal escape from my mouth. Dwight wrapped one arm around my waist and dropped his other hand between my legs. I felt my body explode and stifled a scream. I'd never experienced anything like it before. Fast and furious. As Dwight climaxed, we collapsed on the bath-room floor in a panting heap. We put ourselves back together not saying a word. When we rose from the floor, we stood nose to nose.

"Hello Sarah," Dwight said with a smile.

"Hello, Dwight," I said, kissing the tip of his nose. He opened the bathroom door and let me out first.

I found Marie hanging up her cell phone. "I was just trying to call you. Where did you go?"

"Long story!" I said, adjusting my skirt.

"Your lipstick is all over your face."

Dwight came over to the table to take our order and my lipstick was all over his face, too.

Marie looked from one of us to another. All she said was "Nice!"

I reached into my purse again and brought out another tissue. This time I handed it to Dwight, indicating he should wipe his face off. He took the cue and excused himself for a moment.

When he returned, Marie ordered the salmon special for both of us. As we ate, she continued explaining her story. The woman in the local book club Marie had joined became her lover. She was also married and wasn't willing to leave her husband. It started off innocently enough, but soon they were going out after the book club for coffee or ice cream. Then they began to meet before book club to discuss the current topic with each other, before hearing all the babbling women's points of view. One night they took a long walk. Both had seen the same Lifetime movie. Before long, they were confessing their attraction to one another. They began skipping the weekly club and heading for a small motel nearby. It became more difficult. Marie was ready to tell the world she was gay, but her lover wasn't willing to risk it. They decided not to see each other anymore.

Marie told David about her sexual preference, which didn't seem to surprise him. He didn't want Marie to leave him and came up with what he considered the perfect solution. He suggested that he would continue to dress in women's underwear, and she could pretend he was a girl! Marie explained to him that he was missing the point. All that was left were the divorce papers and the custody agreement regarding Emily, her fifteen-year-old daughter. She wasn't worried about Oliver and Mason. Oliver, a successful architect had his own apartment. Mason was in college. Marie wanted to move back to Marin to be closer to her parents.

As I listened to Marie's story, I felt a disconnect. Maybe it was because my feelings were hurt that she hadn't included me in her identity crisis and everything she was going through. At the same time, my mind was pre-occupied by what had just taken place in the bathroom. I was shocked by the passion that had risen in me. I felt as if Dwight's cock was still inside me. For the first time in my life, I actually felt connected to the power of my sexuality. Odd to think a handicap bathroom had something to do with it.

Marie continued to speak, trying to explain to me the huge decisions she was making. "I feel completely emancipated, like I'm finally living in my truth."

"Well, I think that's wonderful, Marie. I really do." I wanted to support her, "Are you seeing anyone at the moment?"

Marie shook her head. "I think I need time for myself right now, you know? It feels like I'm on some spiritual journey. In fact, after Thanksgiving, I'm taking a month and going to India!!"

"India?" I asked. "Why India?"

"This time it was Oprah. You see, there was this book . . . " she began.

"*Eat, Pray, Love*?" I interrupted, knowing the answer.

"Yes! Oh my God, have you read it?"

I didn't have the heart to tell her I couldn't get through the book. I felt the whole going off to chant somewhere a little dated.

"I'm going to an Ashram then on to work in an orphanage."

"Wow. Cool!!" I responded, trying to seem sincere.

We finished and another server came to the table, a young woman this time. "Do you ladies want coffee?"

"Where's Dwight?" I asked.

"He's on his break."

Marie and I declined the caffeine and asked for the bill. Needless to say, the two of us fought over who would cover it. Marie won and paid.

As we walked out, she asked if she could bring anything with her on Thanksgiving. I suggested wine, and it occurred to me, I should invite her brother, Terry. "Is your brother going to be with your mother for Thanksgiving? He is more than welcome to join us."

"Mother will be in Aspen with her girlfriends for the holiday. I'm sure Terry would love to come. I'll ask him. You know he's always had a huge crush on you!" Marie confessed.

"No, you just imagined it."

"Are you kidding? I found little love notes he had written to you when he was ten years old." She laughed.

I was surprised that she was aware of that information. At the top of the stairs that led to the parking lot I saw something that made my heart stop. Dwight was at the bottom of the stairs with his arms wrapped around a delicately pretty, young, woman. He spotted us and casually waved. "Hey ladies. Meet my fiancée, Violet."

I don't remember much other than my flesh marrying concrete. Dwight broke my fall as I toppled down the stairs.

God, I hate hospitals. This visit was particularly humiliating. The only thing broken was the heel of my sexy Dolce and Gabana shoe. I did need a couple of stitches in my forehead. Dwight's teeth and my head had connected on the flight down the stone steps of Stone Manor. Fortunately, the wound was at my hairline, so my bangs could cover any unsightly scar. I sat behind curtain number one and he and his fiancee behind number two. I was barely aware of the pain in my head, but the wound in my heart was hemorrhaging. I was feeling vulnerable to say the least. I had just had sex with this guy in a bathroom, and minutes later he is introducing me to the girl he's going to marry? I didn't know whether to laugh or cry. Well, I suppose I have to chalk it up to maturity. After all, I am so much older. I should've known better.

I had to keep Marie from giving Dwight an ear full. She was determined to go behind his curtain and yell at him. To add insult to injury, we left the hospital before Dwight was discharged, and Violet was standing outside smoking a cigarette. As we passed, she asked me for an autograph. She had read all of my books. Oy!

Marie drove me home from the emergency room. I learned that not much had been done to Dwight's split lip, but his two "perfect" front teeth were loose and he needed to see a dentist soon to avoid losing them. I intended to knock them out of his head first. We pulled up in front of my house, and I thanked Marie for hanging in with me all night.

"What are best friends for, dummy. Thank you for listening and understanding . . . "

"Geez, of course!"

She offered to pick me up in the morning to get my car, which was still at Stone Manor. I promised to call her when I woke up. At the hospital, they had prescribed a few nice, warm, and friendly pain pills I was intending to use. I was hoping to have a long, deep sleep. I could feel my middle-aged body aching as I climbed out of Marie's car at two in the morning.

Manuel was sitting in the living room alone when I entered the house. He stood when he saw the bandage on my forehead, "Miss Sarah!! What happened?"

I explained that it was nothing and that I would be as right as rain in the morning. I was more concerned about why he was up so late by himself?

He looked at the ground and tried to hide the tears that collected in the creases of his eyes. "Your mother? She didn't know me this night!"

Instinctively, I put my arms around him. "It's the disease, Manuel," I explained. "And it will get worse. Where is she now?"

He told me he had taken her to bed a couple of hours ago, but she fought him every step of the way. I suggested we both get some sleep and promised to look in on mother once upstairs.

I padded into my parent's room. It was dark with the exception of a small Tiffany lamp on the bedside table.

"Sarah? Is that you?"

"Yes, Ma. It's me." I walked over to the side of the bed.

"Where's Manuel?" She asked.

"He's gone to bed," I answered, happy that she remembered him.

"Lie down with me, Sarah."

I kicked off my remaining shoe and climbed in next to her. Not since Phoebe's birth had we lain side by side. Not once did I recall her ever holding me close to her. She had never been overly affectionate, even before Rachel's death. She wasn't the snuggly kind. As she turned to face the wall, my arms automatically wrapped around her, and we formed mother- daughter spoons. She smelled like baby powder and lemon soap. I was given a pain pill at the hospital and had intended to take another pill once home, but Mother fell fast asleep in no time and I drifted shortly after.

I awoke, in my mother's bed, still clothed. I had slept so soundly that I didn't hear her leave the room. As I stretched, I was caught off guard by how much my body ached. "Oh, my God," I said aloud. I tested various body parts to see if one area of my body might be pain free. I felt as if I had collided with a train. Well, I had fallen down a flight of stone steps. I lifted myself slowly and cautiously from the bed. While I was painfully easing myself toward the study, I noticed a journal resting on the pillow next to mine with a small, handwritten note sitting on top.

Sarah,

Please read someday.

Love Mom.

I picked up the book and flipped through the pages. They were in Mother's handwriting. A quick glance revealed dated entries from the sixties up until the eighties. It looked as if Mother had given me a key that might unlock some of the secrets of her world. I felt honored that she was sharing her private thoughts and feelings. I was a bit nervous about what she might have said about her feelings for me. The idea of learning who Olivia Mancuso O'Malley really was intrigued me. I clutched the journal to my breast as I left the room.

I heard the sound of a vacuum cleaner downstairs, indicating that Vilma, the housekeeper, was here as always on Tuesdays. Only two days remained 'til Thanksgiving with so much to do.

The door to Henry's old room was open at the end of the hallway. My dad had converted this room for Mother to work on her hobbies. Dad thought it would be nice for her to have her own space. She painted and glue gunned just about everything in sight. She was very into it for a while. She made Christmas wreaths for our neighbors. She would sit in her garden and paint the flowers then turn the little gems into greeting cards. A local store actually carried a few of her creations, and she was pleased with herself anytime something sold. She was happy, almost at peace with herself. After a few years that all changed. Her depression seemed to kick in again. She used the room less and less. Her paint brushes dried out into a crusty wasteland of unrealized potential.

When I poked my head in the door of Henry's old room, I saw Manuel and my mother inflating an air bed on the floor. "Hey guys," I said. They both looked up. I asked what they were doing.

"My grandchildren are coming to stay you know," my mother stated proudly.

Manuel added, "We make up this room for one of the girls and Vilma is fixing the room near kitchen."

"Wow. That's great. Thank you!" I realized I hadn't even thought of where my children would be sleeping. "Thank you, Manuel."

"Me too!! Me too!!" my mother insisted.

"Of course, you too, Mom."

I planned my day around getting everything from Phoebe's list for Thanksgiving dinner and picking up my car from the restaurant. I was supposed to stop by the hospital to have the bandage changed, but I figured I could do it myself. How difficult could it be, after all? Lily was flying in with the boyfriend first thing in the morning. Phoebe was driving from San Francisco.

It occurred to me that maybe my mother would like to get out and go to the market with me. I was surprised she said she would love to go. "Well, you better get a sweater, Mom, it's chilly out."

My mother stood in front of me scanning my face. It appeared that she either didn't hear me or didn't quite know what I had said.

"A sweater?" I repeated. "It's cold outside."

"Oh, yes," my mother replied as if surprised.

I grabbed a yogurt and thanked Vilma for helping make up the room next to the kitchen. Manuel entered from the backyard, and I asked him if he would take me to pick up my car so that I could go to the market. "Mom said she wants to come, too."

"That is good Miss Sarah!" He still seemed depressed that mother had not remembered who he was. I texted Marie and told her that I was covered for picking up my car and thanked her again. I put the phone away and looked up just as mother walked back into the kitchen. She was dressed, from head to toe, in full gardening regalia. She had on her wide brimmed hat and her Wellington boots over her tucked in overalls. Her tool belt holding her gardening sheers and mini shovel was strapped around her waist.

"Oh, Manuel," she said. "There you are. I missed you last night."

I could see Manuel's relief that her memory was back . . . for a while at least.

"Sarah and I are going shopping," she said gleefully. I figured it wasn't worth commenting about the outfit. We piled into Mom's car, Manuel at the wheel, and headed down the road.

Once I picked up my car and we got to the market, Mother decided to leave the tool belt in the car. Twenty years ago, I probably would have been beside myself with embarrassment to be seen with my mother looking like Mr. Greenjeans. I found it rather endearing at this time in our lives.

I had been in the produce section, maybe ten minutes, before I realized my mother was MIA. I thought she was getting the Brussels sprouts, but as I scanned the produce section, she was nowhere in sight. "Oh no!" I said out loud. I began racing my cart and looking down all the aisles. On reaching the end of the market with no sight of her, I stopped and asked a stock clerk if he'd seen an elderly woman dressed like a gardener. The young man smiled and said that he saw her walk out of the market about ten minutes earlier.

"Oh shit!" I said. I ditched my cart and ran out of the market. My sense of panic turned into sheer terror. I ran to my car, thinking that maybe she was there, but she wasn't. I headed out toward the street. I called for her. "Mother? . . . Olivia O'Malley? Where are you?" I stood, hoping to hear her answer. I turned and walked the other direction toward the rear of the market. Just as I was reaching for my phone to dial 911, I spotted her large hat bobbing up and down, near the dumpsters. I ran over to her on the verge of tears. She was kneeling down feeding the birds an old bag of bread she'd taken from the trash.

"Mother! For Christ's sake, what are you doing? You can't just leave the market like that! I didn't know where you were!!" My voice cracked with emotion.

"Well, I'm right here, Sarah. Feeding the birds!!" she answered reasonably.

Manuel picked mother up from the market and took her home. I returned to the store hoping to find my shopping cart where I'd left it. Wishful thinking. My cart and the twenty-pound turkey I had staked my claim to were nowhere to be found. I started over. Luckily the butcher had a couple of smaller turkeys that weren't frozen. I took those. We'd roast two birds not one big one . . . that way we have double the drumsticks. It would look as if I had planned it all along. The market was packed with frantic pre-holiday shoppers. No one looked at one another. Everyone seemed to be grabbing for the same items at the same time. Stuffing mixes, pumpkin puree, pie crusts, oh my.

Tears poured from my eyes. I was startled at how fast the emotion surfaced. Normally, I might begin with a slight chin quiver or a lump in my throat. Sometimes a golf ball size knot in my stomach would be a sign of impending tears. None of that happened. It was a spontaneous outburst. I just fell apart with no warning in the raw meat section. It was apparent that my mother was disappearing quickly. What if she had walked away and I hadn't found her? Oh, Dear Lord. The last thing I wanted to be doing was marketing for nearly three hours. The panic was interrupted from the joyful beep from my phone indicating I had a text. It was from Dwight.

"Hope ur head's better; Sry bout that. Lol. xxoo"

"What an ass!" I said out loud and cried a little more. Why did I even feel anything for this guy? I wondered if the fall was some sort of karma, because I was old enough to be his mother? My spirit guides pushed me down the stairs to save me from myself. I stood in the checkout line sniffling, mascara streaming down my face. I texted back "Fuck Off." And just like that . . . it was finished. I was now free to concentrate on the matters at hand . . . my mother and Thanksgiving. Baby steps, baby steps.

I pulled into mother's driveway to find a bright pink Jaguar sitting there. The license plate read "MFF DVR." Sitting behind the wheel of my car, I spelled out what I thought it meant. "Ahhhh. Muff Diver! Must be my agent, Sybil!" No one else would be so bold.

Manuel came out and began to unload my car, so I went into the house where I found my mother and Sybil playing cards in the living room. I hadn't seen Sybil in about a year. We mostly communicated via e-mail or on the phone. I was taken aback by her shock of pink hair and the small jewel pierced into her prominent nose.

"Sarah . . . darling," she exclaimed as she stood to greet me. Sybil stood five feet nine. Her beak-like nose protruded between her large, green, Tammy Faye eyes. She resembled a large heron out of a Lewis Carroll novel or a Tim Burton dream. She stretched out her "wings" to embrace me. Sybil had been my biggest fan from the beginning. She loved my work and was the greatest support system when I believed I couldn't write another word. She stuck with me. It obviously paid off for her, too. Fifteen best sellers later and a brand new Jaguar.

"I didn't expect you 'til tomorrow!" I said, as she squeezed the life from me.

"Thought I'd get a jump on things. See if I could help you out with anything," she answered.

"I see you and Mother have bonded."

"She doesn't remember me," Sybil whispered in my ear.

"I know," I whispered back.

"Finish the game with me Sybil," my mother called out.

"Sure thing, Mrs. O'Malley." Sybil winked at me and sat back down on the couch. "Your deal."

I went to help Manuel put the groceries away in the kitchen, but he had everything under control. I asked him if my mother had commented at all about the market incident, but he said she didn't say a word on the way home.

"You know, Manuel," I began, "we may need to think about finding a place for her."

"Oh no, Miss Sarah, I can take care of her. She will be fine!" There was panic in his voice.

I chose not to continue the discussion, but I knew in my heart that after the holiday I would have to begin the task of finding an alternative place for my mother for her own safety.

When my mother and Sybil finished their card game, which Sybil let her win, my agent asked me to go with her to one of her favorite bars in town so we could talk. Having been gone all day, I was hesitant at first, but she promised it was only fifteen minutes away. It was late in the day and dinner time was approaching. Manuel insisted he had everything under control on the home front. I asked if we could bring anything back. He told me that Vilma had made tamales and that he would make an apple pie. I should go and have a good time. No wonder my mother loved him.

Sybil drove like a maniac. It was like being in a car with Mario Andretti during the Indy 500. She gunned each curve and took pride at how fast her car would go on the straight-away. "Wanna put the top down?" She asked as we banked another curve.

"No thanks," I said, feeling more car sick with each hairpin turn. We pulled into a quiet street, lined mostly with homes and trees. At the end of the street were a pizza parlor, a liquor store, and a bar called "Pink Fruits." As I wobbled out of her Indy car, I looked around and said, "I never knew this place was here."

"Been around for years," Sybil replied, hooking her arm through mine. When we walked in, everyone knew Sybil. The bartender called out her name, and the overly buff bouncer did the same. Pink leather booths lined the outer rim of the place. Each booth had its own tiny pink chandelier. The décor was very art deco. A dance floor beckoned in the middle of the room surrounded by cabaret style tables and chairs. A "cigarette girl" in short shorts, carried a tray laden with cigars, cigarettes, and chewing gum. As she passed, I noticed condoms, too. We were escorted, by a pretty young thing, to a booth where Sybil ordered two pink Margaritas. Looking around, I realized the bar was filled with same sex couples.

"This a gay bar?" I was caught off guard.

"Give the lady a cigar!" Sybil laughed. "I brought you here to tell you something. I've decided to leave the business. I am retiring early."

My heart sank, and I couldn't keep myself from groaning, "Oh no!"

"I just don't want to be some old, drooling dyke who hasn't seen the world!"

She assured me that she wouldn't do anything until my new book was published and until I had met and accepted the agent she thought should take over representing me.

I knew I should say something, but I couldn't. Sybil was turning my life upside down. I began to feel a little woozy. Was it still that car ride or maybe the drink was stronger than I thought?

"Look, Sarah," she continued. "I'm not going anywhere immediately. But I need this . . . for me . . . you know?"

Ultimately, it is all about abandonment issues for me. There was my Mother, Marie's new life, Dwight, and now this. I felt vulnerable and wanted to cry. Sybil and I had practically grown up in the publishing business together.

My first book was accepted after I put it in the mail and miraculously plucked out of the slush pile. The publisher set up a meeting with a literary agent known in the publishing world as The Bulldog. His name was Harry Goldstein. He smoked Cuban cigars and kept a Persian cat in his office. He had a constant cigar plume above his head like just after Wylie Coyote had blown himself up. Sometimes it was hard to take him seriously. Sybil was his receptionist. She was a timid, do-gooder, eager to please. She just wanted to make it in the publishing world and was willing to work around the clock and do almost anything to make a name for herself. Well, almost anything. It didn't matter when I called the office, she was always there.

One day, I had a lunch date with Harry at a trendy sushi place that had just opened. After waiting more than forty-five minutes, I was getting ready to leave. Sybil arrived, breathless. She sat down and told me that Harry couldn't make it. Harry had suffered a heart attack and was in the hospital. I asked her to sit with me and offered her lunch.

She began to cry. She was concerned that she may have had something to do with Harry's heart attack. She cried even harder. I asked her why she would think something like that. She took a deep breath and explained that on many occasions, Harry would call her into his office, lock the door, and force himself on her. He never got very far. She always managed to fight him off, but he was relentless. After she told him she was a lesbian, he became more persistent. She reached a point where she couldn't take it anymore. She did the only thing she could think of. She hired a lawyer, mostly to threaten him. She just wanted him to leave her alone. Instead, he had a heart attack.

I tried to reassure her that it wasn't her fault at all. I reminded her that he smoked furiously and was obese. It was only a matter of time until something like this happened. Bottom line, though, he never should have tried anything inappropriate with her. I suggested she go out on her own, and I said I would be her first client.

Harry retired and sold the business to Sybil for a minimal sum mainly to keep her mouth shut. She inherited all of his clients and the Persian cat as well. It wasn't long before she had made a name for herself as one of the finest literary agents around. So, here we sat, years and many bestsellers later, in our pretty, pink, leather booth, staring at one another.

"Sarah?"

I turn around, and there was Marie, standing behind me. She had her arm around a twenty-something Kate Moss look alike.

"Marie?!" I said, standing to give her a hug. "What are you doing here?" Then I realized. "Oh yeah, now that you're 'out' you're at a gay bar! Silly me." That sounded awful and mean. I didn't mean to say that out loud. She could have asked me the same thing!

Sensing tension, Sybil stood up and promptly stuck out her hand to the girls and introduced herself.

I believe Marie said the girl on her arm was named was Saffron. What kind of name is that, I wondered.

Sybil invited them to join us! I was tempted to yell "no!" They were quick to take up residence. Marie squeezed into my side of the booth with Saffron, so I scooted around to sit next to Sybil. She pinched me under the table, to warn me to be good.

Saffron appeared apoplectic as if she'd been technically knocked out, but hadn't hit the floor yet. Marie was like a speed freak. She spoke a mile a minute about how the two of them had met in the cold and flu section of the pharmacy. It had been instant chemistry between them. Marie giggled.

I was fascinated by Marie's remarkable, seemingly overnight, transformation from being a fairly demure housewife and mother to a gay woman with an adolescent crush. Marie put her arm around the girl and stroked the back of her neck. Saffron didn't utter a word. She was frozen. She reminded me of a fairy or an elf. Something out of *A Midsummer Night's Dream*. Her hair was dark brown with a white blonde streak at the front. Her ears were slightly vulcan-like, and a little pointy at the top. Her eyes resembled Bambi's with huge lashes shading large brown orbs. Her nose had a ski slope flip and her mouth seemed to curl slightly downward, resembling an unhappy, happy-face. She was cute, I'll give her that, but just not the type I would expect Marie to be attracted to. Maybe because she was probably not a day over twenty-two! But then, who am I to talk? I recently had sex with a guy who barely had his driver's license.

Marie and Sybil dominated the conversation the entire hour we sat there. They laughed and drank heavily. When Saffron began to text someone intensely I decided I'd had enough and said I needed to get back to the house. It wasn't really a lie. My family was arriving the next day.

"Oh, Sarah," Marie began as we stood. "About Thanksgiving . . . "

Oh God! I thought. Here it comes. She's going to ask to bring Saffron . . .

"What kind of wine do you want me to bring?"

"Oh, Marie, whatever you want will be fine," I replied, relieved I didn't have to watch the two of them canoodling all day. We all performed the obligatory air kisses as we left the bar. Sybil and I climbed back into the "pink hornet" and sped back down the street.

"Your friend is adorable," Sybil began. "That ain't gonna last by the way . . . Marie and Coriander."

"Saffron!" I corrected her.

"Whatever! Ain't gonna last!" she repeated.

I secretly wanted to agree, but I pretended I didn't hear her instead. I was more focused on not throwing up due to Sybil's driving technique.

When we got back to the house, Sybil was a huge help even though she was snockered. We set a beautiful holiday table, two days early. "You'll want to spend time with the girls . . . not setting the table!" Sybil had suggested. She had noticed the interaction between Manuel and my mother. In her inimitable fashion, she asked, "What's with your mother and Jose Cuervo?"

Trying to give her the edited version, I briefly described the relationship between them, that presumably had gone on for many years.

"Holy shit, Sarah . . . that's an amazing book right there!"

I protested that it wasn't the sort of book I wrote.

"Well," she said, "now's the time to start Sarah! Do something a little more substantial. Write what you know!"

Substantial! I knew that she was trying to be encouraging, but I immediately went to the place of ridicule, abandonment, unworthiness, no talent, uselessness. The sting of her words nearly brought me to my knees. I didn't say anything about my feelings. I knew she meant to encourage and motivate me.

I watched her drive off and head for her hotel around 10 p.m. I knew how much I would miss her being my agent and wasn't sure what I would do without her.

Manuel had tucked mother into bed, so I tiptoed past her room to avoid waking her. No sooner had I walked by her door that I heard her call out to me. I poked my head into her room. She was sitting upright in bed with the small lamp on.

"Read to me Sarah," she said, holding up the journal she had given to me earlier. She must have gone into my room and taken it back sometime during the day.

"I thought you wanted me to read it alone," I said.

"Changed my mind . . . let's read it together."

"Okay." I wasn't sure how to handle this one. God only knows what she had written in these pages. Maybe I would be embarrassed reading out loud. Maybe there would be things about me that would be hurtful to know. I was in a turmoil of emotions and questions. As I climbed up onto the bed next to my mother and she handed me the book, I realized the power of what was happening. Not only did Mother want to share with me, but this was a tangible link to the past for a mind that was quickly evaporating.

I assumed I should start on page one. So I opened the journal and looked over at Mother. She had fallen fast asleep. I set the book down, and switched off her little light. I walked back to my room, relieved that I didn't have to unlock some of the past tonight.

Chapter Eight

I Think We're Gonna Need A Bigger Boat

I awoke the next morning to Manuel's taps on my door. "Miss Sarah? Lily is here," he whispered through the door.

I sat bolt upright and glared at my clock. "9:30 a.m.? What?" I never sleep this late. "I'll be right down Manuel!"

I threw the bedclothes off me. Lily's plane must have landed early. I wondered why she hadn't phoned to tell me. I picked up my cell phone which I had forgotten to charge.

It was out of juice. I quickly brushed my teeth and hair, splashed water on my face, and threw on sweat pants and an old tee shirt. I'd shower later. I was too excited to see Lily.

Lily was standing in the garden with my mother, who was showing her the newest roses. Lily was a beautiful girl. She had inherited Rachel's blonde ringlets. Today she was wearing a flowing, flowered skirt, a tank top, and flip flops, shades of me in the seventies. When I stepped out the back door, she spotted me immediately and a huge smile broke across her face. "Mama!" She cried out, running over to me. We held onto one another for a long time.

Lily and I were always very close. From an early age, Phoebe preferred not to be held too close and would even push me away at times. Lily thrived on being held. She and I were cut from the same cloth, and Phoebe and Brad were more alike. Lily broke away, stood back, and noticed the small bandage on my forehead. "Mom . . . what happened?"

I explained my spill, but left Dwight out of it. "Where's the boyfriend?" I inquired.

"He's washing up. Mom, you're gonna love him . . . Maybe he could look at your head! You know he's a second year resident doctor . . . " she bragged to me for the umpteenth time.

No sooner had we spoken of him than Raj came out into the garden. He was born in the USA, a first generation American of Pakistani parents. His olive skin and green eyes were striking. His six-foot two inch frame seemed to glide across the lawn toward us. I extended my hand, but he embraced me instead.

"Mom, this is Raj," Lily said.

"I see that!"

Raj frowned a little at my bandage.

"It's no big deal. A couple of stitches." I was beginning to feel self conscious.

"Well, I could look at it if you like," Raj offered.

"Mom?" I turned to see Phoebe at the back door. My heart jumped. She looked amazing. Her hair was cropped short and dyed red. Although she was a natural blonde, the red set off the small freckles on her nose and her huge green eyes. She ran toward Lily and me, and we all formed a ring-around-the-rosy embrace. I wasn't prepared for the emotions that swept through me. I had both my girls in my arms at the same time.

"I want to hug, too!" My mother called from behind a bramble bush. When Mother joined in, I could sense her confusion about what we were doing. When we broke the circle, we stood smiling at one another, commenting on each other's hair, shoes, the great weather, Phoebe said she had a surprise. "Now, don't be mad Mom," she warned.

"What is it? The pony I never got as a child?" I laughed watching her disappear back into the house.

Only seconds later, she returned leading a man by the arm. I blinked a few times to make certain I was seeing straight. Phoebe had brought her father . . . Brad!

"Big girls don't cry. Big girls don't cry . . . " rang out in my head before I hit the dirt.

I gather Dr. Raj carried me into the house, laying me on the sofa. He checked my jugular vein for a pulse and made sure my pupils were not fixed and dilated. I could hear Brad's voice swimming in my head. He was commenting on how he thought I had outgrown the fainting spells and couldn't believe it still happened. The voice in my head attacked him "Well, you might know these things if you hadn't wrecked our marriage, you schmuck."

When I opened my eyes, I was surrounded by the entire household. Even Vilma had a glass of water for me. I wondered if I was supposed to drink it or if she was standing by to throw it in my face. I sat up protesting that all was fine . . . low blood sugar . . . I explained. "What are you doing here?" I asked my ex-husband, my words hitting him squarely between the eyes.

"Mom please . . . It's my fault, not Dad's. I asked him to come."

"Well, thanks for the warning," I shot back.

Brad knelt down beside the couch. I scanned his face to see if he had changed. He looked the same as he always had. A few new lines around his mouth and eyes, a crop circle of vanishing hair on top of his head, but he was still quite handsome. "I'm sorry for surprising you, Sarah," he said in a hushed tone. "My life's a mess right now, and I didn't want to be alone over the holiday."

"So what . . . you expect me to take care of you?" Everyone began slowly backing out of the living room, to leave us alone. "Look, Brad. I'm sorry, but honestly, I haven't seen you in ages. We barely speak other than formal e-mails occasionally, and all of a sudden you are in my parents' home acting as though everything is the same between us? How did you think I'd react?"

I waited a second for a reply, but Brad looked down at the floor.

"Things aren't hunky dory for me at the moment either," I said, at which point the flood gates opened and Brad began crying.

"Oh man . . . don't cry!" I thought. I can't resist a crying man.

He collected himself and explained that his little miss muff had left him for a local pediatrician and had withdrawn money from his bank account without his knowledge. Furthermore, his mother had a benign lump removed from her breast, and they had to put her old sheepdog down, too.

"You had to put Sadie down?" I asked with a lump in my throat.

Brad nodded and cried some more.

"God, I loved that dog. Look," I said, sitting up. "It's fine that you're here . . . I just don't want you staying in the house, okay? Find a room somewhere and have Thanksgiving dinner with us. That's fine." Echoing a scene in one of my books, Brad, still kneeling, kissed the back of my hand and thanked me. It reminded me of what I had written years earlier in *The Prince and the Pupil*.

His Highness, still on one knee, took my hand in his and slowly brought it to his lips. I felt my heart fluttering deep within my chest as his lips parted and rested on top of my hand. I felt his moist tongue lightly touching my fingers. Looking around, he made sure no one could tell what was happening, as he flicked his tongue in between my fingers. I was reminded of where he had placed his tongue earlier that day.

It was morning and I sat in my room. I had finished my needle-point the evening before, and I had completed the lesson over an hour ago. As I awaited his arrival, I looked at my assignment one more time. Hearing a tap on my door, I set down my writings.

"Enter," I called out, knowing it was the Prince. I tried to remain calm and very much a lady when I saw him in the doorway. I tried to hide the shivers that raced through my body in anticipation of what I knew was to come.

Closing the door, the Prince walked over to where I was seated. He fell to his knees in front of me. Never uttering a word, he slowly lifted my skirts, high above my waist and pulled my hips toward him. With expert precision, he placed his tongue between my legs. I watched the future King taste me as if I were his last supper.

But this evening in the great hall, we play acted. Sitting on opposite sides of the table neither relishing our meal, we hoped we were lending no suspicion to the true goings on between us. He rose slowly, pushing his plate aside. He looked at me, his eyes beckoning "Come see me later." I noticed the bulge within his riding pants and I knew he was without his codpiece.

Phoebe had vanished into the kitchen to check on all the food. When I joined her she began to apologize again. "Mom, I'm so sorry, dad called and was crying. I didn't know what to do!"

"It's fine, Phoebs," I said. The whole thing was typical of him! Involving his daughter in the drama he created for himself, really pissed me off!

"I just wished you had warned me, that's all. We'll make it work somehow," I told her how happy I was that she and her sister were with me for the Holiday. "Where is Lily by the way?" I asked.

"Chanting."

"Chanting?" I repeated.

"In the garden. With Raj. They chant twice a day. It's a good thing, Mom."

I left the kitchen and began to take stock of the whereabouts of the household. Manuel had gone upstairs, Brad was on his phone in the driveway, Mother was lying down in her room. I stood in the hallway feeling like Alice through the looking glass. Who were these people I call my family?

Brad came in and announced he'd gotten a room at the motor inn.

"That's where my brother is staying," I said.

"I know," Brad replied. "I spoke to him yesterday. He told me."

"You spoke to Henry? How often do you talk to my brother?"

"Not that often . . . maybe once a month."

I was so confused. Why would my ex-husband and my brother communicate that often or at all? Rather than start something, I went back into the kitchen just in time to help Phoebe with some more prep work.

Lily and Raj had resurfaced and were having a snack. "Raj brought homemade brownies for tomorrow," Lily said with pride.

"Yum! Your grandma will be happy. She loves brownies . . . at least if she remembers she does."

"Is Grandma really that bad?" Lily asked.

I nodded and told the girls about losing her at the market, forgetting what her sweater was and other disturbing behavior that had occurred since my stay. "I'm going to begin investigating a few options next week. I want to find a place for grandma, somewhere she can be safe."

Both my daughter's faces registered something. I turned to see my mother standing in the doorway. My heart sank.

"Where do you plan on putting me?" she asked.

"Mom," I stopped, trying to consider what to say. "Nothing has been decided yet." I could tell she wasn't buying it.

"Well, you have to do what you think is right, I suppose," she said and turned to leave. I watched Mother's head drop as she walked away. It was difficult for me to know if she was comprehending what we were thinking or not.

"Oh, dear Lord." I spoke the words out loud. Lily came to me and wrapped her arms around me. I didn't want to cry. I shouldn't cry, but I felt that catch in my throat. "I really don't know what to do!" I whispered into Lily's neck.

The house vibrated all day. Phoebe could be heard in the kitchen, working on her knife skills, chopping her vegetables. Lily had taken Mother into the rose garden and the two of them were gathering flowers for the table centerpiece. Manuel seemed a little out of place, but chopped more wood and stocked the fire place. Raj drove Brad over to the motor inn so he could check in. I was praying Brad wouldn't pry too much about Raj and Lily's relationship. I had to admit, there was a feeling of comfort having all my family together under one roof.

Not long after the sun set, someone decided we should order Chinese food and play charades. Must have been Brad's idea to do the charades considering that is what his life has been! Henry called to say that he had crashed at the motel and would see us tomorrow. Manuel disappeared into the UFO, probably feeling like the outsider.

We sat on the floor in the living room in front of the fire eating out of our to-go boxes with chopsticks. The smell of burning wood and kung pao wafted through the house.

Teams for charades were chosen while I was in the bathroom. I ended up on Brad's team. Swell! It was mother, Lily, and Phoebe against Brad, Raj, and myself . . . two men I hardly know. I drew the number one, which meant I went first. I picked my clue and opened the small piece of paper. "The unbearable lightness of being . . ."

Swell!

I put up my hands in my imaginary book and camera poses.

Brad yelled, "Book . . . and movie!"

I nodded. I held up five fingers.

"Five words!" Brad screamed.

I nodded. I held up two fingers.

"Second word!" Raj joined in.

I nodded. I slapped two fingers on my arm.

"Second word! We know that!! Raj already guessed . . . " Brad was already driving me nuts.

I shook my head no, furiously.

"Two syllables!!" Raj yelled.

I nodded. I again tapped my arm with two fingers.

"Second syllable!" Brad guessed.

I nodded, wanting to kill him. I threw up my hands, positioning them like claws and bared my teeth.

"TIGER! LION! MONSTER! HANNABAL LECTER!" They both screamed at me simultaneously.

Oy . . . This was getting old! I shook my head.

"BEAR!" Raj got it.

I nodded.

"THE UNBEARABLE LIGHTNESS OF BEING!!!" Brad screamed.

I nodded, touching my finger to my nose longing to flip him off with the other hand.

Our team won.

Mother hung in there guessing "Mary Poppins" based on Phoebe trying to look like a jack in the box or someone on a pogo stick. How Mother guessed the right answer from those clues was amazing, but she continued guessing Mary Poppins with every other clue for the rest of the game.

I experienced an unexpected longing for my father in the midst of it all. Though he loathed charades, he was very proficient at the game. I missed my father terribly when I climbed the stairs to my room, to his old room. This Christmas would be three years without him.

The constant beeping noise from the heart monitor almost drove me insane. I couldn't help trying to keep up with the beat of it, tapping my toes, or my fingers, in unison to the little blips. Mother, Henry and I took turns with the Daddy shift. Mother was the morning/late afternoon shift. I took the evening until around ten or eleven, and Henry did the all-nighter. He was a doctor after all and used to those hours.

Dad had been in the hospital for five days. He had suffered another massive heart attack, and this time it didn't look good. He was slack jawed, his mouth wide open, his cheeks sunken, and his skin void of any color. Sometimes his eyes would flutter, and we would get excited, but there was no light behind them. No life force. On May 23rd at 4:30 p.m., on my sentry, Dad opened his eyes and looked right at me.

"Sarah!" he said. His voice was raspy. I had been reading *The Grapes of Wrath* to him. He loved Steinbeck.

"Daddy!!!" I sat on his bed next to him and put my head on his chest. I could hear his heart thumping like a sixteen-year-old. It sounded good.

"Sarah, tell your mother it was always her. No one else . . . only her that I loved." He coughed.

I looked into my father's face. He was fully there. I knew he wasn't delusional or saying things because of the drugs. He was the strong man I had known and loved my whole life. I couldn't hold back my tears.

"I will tell her, Dad."

And then, the ever-present beeping turned into a single long note. I held my dad and I could feel him go. He suddenly became lighter in my arms as if he had left his body.

"Oh God, Dad, please not yet!!!" I called to him. Almost as soon as I asked him not to go, I felt his body drop back into himself. He became heavy in my arms again and breathed in a huge breath. He was back! Once again the monitor beeped, and he opened his eyes. A nurse had quietly slipped in.

"Looks like he wasn't quite ready," she said and smiled. Dad looked at me again. "I love you, Sarah," he said. A wonderful peacefulness appeared on his face. "You and Henry have made me proud . . . " He paused. "I saw Rachel . . . an angel." And with that, he closed his eyes, never to open them again.

I called my mother and Henry. I could tell by my mother's voice that she resented that dad had departed on my watch. When Henry and Mother arrived at the hospital mother went into his room first. Looking stoic as usual, she entered and stayed for almost an hour. If she cried, we never saw it.

Although one hears how difficult it is losing a parent obviously no one knows how it will affect you until it actually happens. Seventy years old seemed ancient to me when I was younger. Now that I am closer to that number myself, it seems unfair that my dad went at that age. Over the years we had become much closer. Having children of my own made it easier for me to understand and accept his foibles. When he finally passed I think we had come to the basic understanding that we loved each other and he did the best that he could as a father.

I had been to several funerals, beginning, of course, with Rachel's. The day of his funeral was perfect. The scent of rosemary and lavender perfumed the air. Dad would have loved it. The sun was high in the sky with only a few wispy clouds. We were relieved that Mother had chosen not to have an open casket, mostly because dad would have hated that. So many people came from his past and present to say their farewells. Mother was gracious in welcoming everyone and assumed the role of the grieving widow perfectly.

As dad was about to be laid to rest next to Rachel, I noticed a lone figure, standing a slight distance from us watching the proceedings. It was Helen. She looked so old and frail. When she and my father had their affair, she must have been quite a bit older than he.

In the early days I had done a book of erotic vignettes titled *Hot Chocolate and Stilettos*. One was about the older woman/younger man scenario . . .

Who knew back then that I would find myself having amazing sex with someone who may not even know who The Beatles were. My father acted out his scenario with Helen and now I was playing out a similar dynamic with Dwight.

The Musician's Mistress . . .

It had been entirely her fault and she knew it. She had only herself to blame that her heart had been shattered into dust. She couldn't help being drawn to the young musician with the dancing eyes. When he spoke, the words were melodies to her ears. She had been a slave to her marriage, giving everything she had to a man who only wanted to control her. She bore his five beautiful children, kept an immaculate house, prepared fine dinners each night. The love that she felt early on had become a distant memory. She knew that he lusted for other women, while she hungered for love.

When she was with the young man who had captured her attention many months ago, she never wanted to leave. They sat close to one another, uncertain in these uncharted waters. It wasn't proper for a Southern woman to be alone with a man who wasn't her husband. The world was different now, she justified. Life for all those around changed that day when President Kennedy was killed. There had been a tangible shift on the planet and in her heart. She threw caution to the wind, realizing how short life is.

After graduating Julliard, the musician found himself in many places for short periods of time. Being first violinist for the New York Philharmonic was quite a commitment. The young protégé brought a lot of attention to the orchestra.

This had been the longest length of stay on the tour. He liked the South. After meeting her that night, he grew to love it even more.

How does one explain an instant connection? All the two of them knew was that when they first looked into each other's eyes it was as if they had known one another before. He had slipped his number at the hotel to her that first night. He couldn't believe he had been so brazen, but he worried he might never see her again. He was surprised when she called two days later.

For her, their meeting had a powerful effect. She didn't know why she would call a young man she had only just met to plan a clandestine meeting. This was not something she ever imagined doing.

They had several meetings—the park, the diner, and then finally his hotel room.

When he slipped his hand into hers, she felt a spark that charged all of her senses. He leaned into her, and their lips touched. His were soft, not rough. They rendered her breathless. As their tongues met, it was a new language for them both.

He had longed to be inside her for days. He would wake in the night with lustful thoughts of her. The stiffness he felt beneath the covers each night was nearly unbearable. And now, here she was, beside him. He wanted to savor each moment . . . each sensation. He wanted to hear how she breathed, to see how her face looked in ecstasy. Slowly, he lifted her blouse and exposed her breasts. He moved his lips and tongue across her nipples, and she gasped. He pressed himself against her thigh making her aware of his manhood beneath his pants. She stroked him evoking a deep moan. His hand slipped between her legs. Hiking up her skirt, he could feel the moistness of her passion. He peeled her panties off and began to tenderly caress her mound. Like the musician he was, he played her as if she was an instrument. His fingers moved over her as if he was playing his violin.

She had never been touched this way before. It drove her crazy. Unable to control herself, she felt a wave of sensations building with each breath. A crescendo of passion welled inside her. Something began to happen. Her body was doing things she had never experienced. With each touch, each chord he seemed to be playing, her body responded powerfully, her breath stopped and suddenly she burst into an internal flame of ecstasy. She floated on wave after wave with this ocean of sensations.

Once she could breathe again, he mounted her and slipped himself inside her. They moved in unison. Both home now. Melting into one. She watched him watching her. Their eyes locked. Each a silent mirror.

Their love making was like a drug. They wanted and needed more. Alas, it could never be.

I awoke to the sound of rain and mouthwatering aromas from the kitchen. Phoebe had been up since dawn working on the Thanksgiving feast. My brother and Brad showed up together around noon, like BFF's. They were three hours early, which was fine for Henry, but I could have done without my ex-husband milling around. To make matters worse, they talked about how they had hung out at the motel bar all night! It bugged me that Brad was insinuating himself back into my family. I couldn't react. I had to keep myself in check, if only for a few hours. At least Mother was happy to see Henry. That took a little of the sting away.

At two, Sybil's pink panther pulled into the driveway. Someone was in the passenger's seat, and I wondered whom she was bringing without telling me. I squinted to try to see better when Sybil turned and kissed her passenger. When they got out of the car and began to sprint toward the front door, I saw that Sybil had just locked lips with Marie. What the.? I was shaken. I quickly weighed my options. Should I accost the two of them as soon as they came in from the torrential rain and ask "What's going on with the two of you?" Or, should I take a deep breath and restrain myself until a more appropriate moment later in the day? Or, maybe I could get Marie alone in the bathroom and pull each hair out of her head slowly. No question, I had to wait.

Robert and Terry arrived in separate cars at the same time. Robert had his familiar trusty umbrella, but Terry got drenched. He resembled a drowned rat by the time he made it into the house. I didn't understand why a man, who would take the time putting on beautifully tailored three piece suit and Hermes tie wouldn't bring an umbrella.

Manuel offered to get Terry a change of clothes and to hang his wet ones up to dry.

Appetizers were on hand for about an hour as people mingled. Phoebe had made Mozzarella and tomato skewers with a balsamic glaze. And crudités, with three different dipping sauces. As a gift, Robert contributed Beluga Caviar and blinis to the feast. Heaven.

Mother was confused by the appetizer thing. She kept asking where the turkey was. Manuel did his best to placate her, but after a while he looked at me and shook his head as if to say, "I don't know what to do!"

Watching all these different people under our roof had me feeling slightly out of body. Everyone seemed more than comfortable. I was the only one climbing out of my skin!

Lily sat on Raj's lap near the fire. Brad and Henry were locked in football conversation. I could tell Marie was cautious about Sybil's attention in front of her father, who looked shell-shocked, to say the least. Terry wound up in the kitchen helping Phoebe. Judging from bursts of laughter from them, I would say they were having a good time.

Once we finally got to the dining room, a demi-cup of roasted chestnut soup was at each place setting as an *amuse bouche*. There were two perfectly browned turkeys, each on its own platter surrounded by roasted potatoes and root vegetables. A gorgeous winter salad sat beside each plate and a steaming gravy boat took center stage near the turkeys. Lily had hand painted little place cards, and people walked around the table looking for their names. I saw Sybil change her card with Terry's so she could be next to Marie. Mother picked her card up and tried to stick it on her sweater.

"Mom, it's not a name tag," Henry said.

"It has my name on it?"

"Yes, Mom, it does, but it is just to let you know where you are to sit."

"Why do I have to know where to sit? I know where to sit!" And she seated herself in the chair that had been marked as Robert's. No one minded the musical chair routine. As long as this day made Mother happy, I knew we all would be happy.

When Phoebe emerged from the kitchen everyone applauded her for making this all happen. Manuel poured red wine into everyone's glasses, and we all toasted the chef and all the people who couldn't be with us.

Robert insisted on carving the turkeys, which he did with utter precision.

Half way through the meal Brad asked, "Who's that in the driveway?"

Everyone turned to look out the window. A man stood in the rain looking at us.

"Oh my God!" I couldn't suppress my response.

"Isn't that your waiter?" Marie asked with a mischievous grin on her face. I shot her a look that could kill.

"Your waiter? What does that mean??" Brad asked.

I excused myself to see what Dwight thought he was doing. I heard the buzz in the room get louder behind me.

Phoebe said, "He's cute."

"Watch it Phoebes! He's your mom's," Marie joked.

"What does that mean?" Brad asked, concerned.

"Oh, I recognize him now . . . " Terry began explaining that he was the waiter at the table the night he and I had had dinner at Stone Manor.

"You and my Mom went out for dinner?" Phoebe asked.

I wanted the ground to swallow me up. I couldn't believe that Dwight would have the nerve to show up during my holiday meal, especially after I had told him to take a hike a few days before.

I opened the front door, and Dwight and I were face-to-face.

"What are you doing here Dwight?"

"I'm sorry, Sarah, I just needed to see you," he said, drops falling from the hat he was wearing. We both stood looking at one another under the front door eve. His eyes were bloodshot, and his nose was red. He'd clearly been crying. For some reason, I felt sorry for him. I was still angry at him for not telling me he was engaged, and I was annoyed that he would show up in the middle of Thanksgiving dinner. I still felt sorry for him.

It was very cold, the rain was getting harder, and I have always been a sucker for a lost puppy. And that is what Dwight reminded me of. I invited him in and pointed him upstairs to my room. I said I would get him a change of clothes. Two drenched guys in one day? What are the odds?

Brad was at my side in no time. The two of us watched Dwight's cute butt saunter upstairs. "Who is that?" Brad asked through clenched teeth.

"A friend of mine," I said looking Brad straight in the eye. He obviously knew what kind of friend I was referring to. Game over.

"God . . . what is he, fifteen?" He snorted.

"Don't you dare, Brad . . . I'll kick you out of this house faster than an atomic blast. Now sit your sorry ass back down at the table and enjoy your daughter's wonderful food and shut up!" I couldn't believe those words came out of my mouth! But, man, it felt good!

I grabbed one of Henry's sweat outfits from the hall closet and went upstairs. When I opened the door to my room, I was greeted by the sound of the shower. "Dwight?" I called into the bathroom. "Um- what are you doing?"

"Oh, hi, Sarah . . . hope you don't mind . . . I was freezing!" He reached outside the shower and grabbed my arm. "Come here, you." He pulled me off my feet.

I kinda, sorta, tried to fight him off, but I knew he'd get me in there one way or another. I pulled my slip dress over my head and climbed into the shower with him. We stood under the warm water staring at one another.

"I think I love you, Sarah . . . "

"No you don't, Dwight," I insisted.

"No . . . really . . . I think I do!! You're all I think about. I can't sleep, I don't eat . . . "

I pulled him close to me and held him tightly. I could smell his familiar scent. A sort of musty, nutty blend. Add a little rain to that, and I couldn't resist. Here's to pheromones. In those few seconds, I wasn't angry anymore. I just felt badly for him. My heart was bursting. It had been a long time since I heard a man tell me he loved me. It felt pretty darn good, even if he was delusional. I wondered if I was in some kind of mid-life crisis, but I threw total caution to the wind anyway. Why was I allowing this young man to get under my skin? Okay, he was a gorgeous specimen of a man. He certainly pleased me in bed. I hadn't had this kind of sexual passion in years. Which undoubtedly explains the attraction.

He told me not only did he tell his fiancé, Violet, that he was in love with someone else, but he also told his mother . . . who instantly uninvited him to Thanksgiving dinner. Violet seemed relieved, he said. She had begun to question whether it was a good idea to get married so young. His mother had other ideas. Violet was from a wealthy family and she had hoped Dwight would not have to work as a waiter much longer.

"Look Dwight . . . I have a house full of guests downstairs, who are probably wondering where I am about now. Get out of the shower, get dressed, and join us down stairs. We can talk about everything else later." I kissed him on the nose and got out.

Everyone knew that something had gone on upstairs. After all, I was wearing a completely different outfit, my hair was wet and my make-up had been washed away.

"Guess you're not in Kansas anymore, eh?" Sybil laughed at me.

Phoebe gave me a thumbs up. Marie shook her head lovingly and smiled. Brad looked as though he might kill someone. Mother didn't notice that I had been gone at all.

Most of the wine had been consumed and both turkeys had been picked clean by the time Dwight got to the table. When he walked into the dining room, everyone fell silent. He looked adorable, wearing sweatpants and a tee shirt and rosy from the shower and from crying.

"Everyone, this is my friend Dwight," I said. Like an A. A. meeting, everyone answered in unison, "Hi Dwight!"

I wanted to shoot myself. Instead, I put a plate of food together for him.

Phoebe asked for help with the desserts, and Manuel jumped up to help her. They set two pecan pies, two pumpkin pies, Raj's brownies and a variety of cookies on the table. Everyone seemed to be watching as Dwight began to eat.

Noticing this, he laughed and said, "I know it's unusual for me to be this side of a table. Usually I'm standing and not eating."

Sybil roared.

"You should enjoy yourself!" Marie chirped.

There was much discussion as to which dessert to have and how much. Terry had brought a nice dessert wine, which we opened.

Robert put a pot of coffee on, and Mother brought the cream and sugar to the table. The food had been pretty much demolished. I was not looking forward to what the kitchen might look like. Dwight offered to help clean up when the time was right.

As the day wore on and people were sufficiently stuffed, everyone seemed to be getting a little frisky. Sybil and Marie were definitely up to something, probably groping each other under the table. Terry and Phoebe seemed to be getting a little cozy, too! Maybe the wine was going to everyone's head.

"So, Dwight?" Brad couldn't contain himself any longer. "How do you know my wife?"

"Ex-wife, Brad . . . in case you forgot."

To his everlasting credit, Dwight stood his ground. "Sarah and I met at Stone Manor a few weeks ago, where I work. I think she is one of the most beautiful, honest, gracious women I have ever met!"

Talk about the proverbial pin drop. There was a stunned silence for at least a minute.

I surprised myself by what I did. I got up from my chair, walked over to him, and kissed him meaningfully on the lips. "Thank you," I whispered to him.

"Right on!" Sybil applauded.

"Sweet!" Lily added.

"Where's grandma?" Phoebe asked. We all realized that no one had seen Mother in at least twenty minutes. Manuel, who had been in the kitchen with Terry, said he would look upstairs. Phoebe would check the bathroom.

Raj stood up with a brownie in his hand. "I don't know how to say this . . . but it appears that I brought the wrong brownies!"

"How can a brownie be wrong???" Marie asked, giggling. "I had two. They were amazing!"

"No, Raj . . . how could that be?" Lily asked with a concerned look on her face.

"Will someone please explain what's going on?" I asked.

"Mom, please don't get angry, but I think what Raj is saying is that these particular brownies have medical marijuana in them!"

"Holy shit!" Henry put his head in his hands. "Mom's had around three of them!"

Sybil did a spit take. Marie giggled some more. It hit me that my mother was probably stoned out of her mind somewhere.

Manuel ran back downstairs shaking his head. "She's not upstairs!"

Without another word spoken, everyone systematically fanned out searching for her. We looked all over the house calling her name to no avail. The rain had intensified. No one wanted to think that mother had left the house, but it was becoming evident that she had.

"Where would she go?" Henry asked.

"I can't imagine." I answered. "She not only has Alzheimer's, but she's just ingested a substantial sized portion of pot! She could be anywhere!"

We decided to drive around the neighborhood looking for her. I asked the girls to stay behind in case she showed up. Raj and Terry offered to stay with them. Robert said he would drive and Brad and Henry offered to go with him. Dwight, Marie and Sybil came with me. Manuel wasn't sure what to do, but thought it would be good for someone to be on foot. He grabbed an umbrella and began walking in the storm toward the street. Armed with our cell phones, each of us clamored into the different cars calling out to one another to call if they spotted her. I made a left out of the driveway, Robert went to the right. The windshield wipers could barely keep up with the pounding rain. Beads of panic sweat formed on my brow. Dwight, who was in the front seat next to me, wiped my forehead dry.

"Maybe one of us should drive, Sarah," Sybil said, aware of the state I was in.

"Thanks, but I'm okay," I replied. The last thing I wanted was Sybil behind the wheel careening through the rain. "I'm getting used to searching for my mother."

We went over the events leading up to Mother's disappearance to see if something had triggered her to take off.

"When you guys were upstairs, your mother started to call Lily . . . Rachel. No one corrected her," Marie said.

"Mom said she has been seeing Rachel lately. She goes down to the cul de sac and sits on the bench. But I looked at the bench as we left the driveway. She wasn't there."

"I know I am the outsider and all," Dwight spoke up, "but where is this Rachel she's taking about? Maybe she went to wherever Rachel is?"

Brilliant, Dwight! "I think you are right." I made a complete 180 turn with a screech and headed in the other direction. "Marie, call your dad. Tell him I'm heading for the cemetery."

The security guard at the mouth of Billings and O'Ryan cemetery was fast asleep in his cubicle. He claimed not to have seen anyone dip under the security arm. He certainly would've noticed an elderly lady on foot, in this rain. I explained what was going on and that we had family members buried on the hill. He lifted the arm of the security gate and let us in.

"How could your mother make it this far?" Dwight asked.

It was only two blocks from the house, but the trek up the hill toward the grave site was a little torturous. "I have no clue Dwight," I said. "It's not as though anything mother does now is within the norm."

Shivers ran down my back as the thought came to me that this day was like the day of Rachel's funeral. The rain, my run up this hill trying to get to the top . . .

As our cars rounded the road, I could spot the graves. A dark shadow was lying on the ground ahead.

"Oh God," I said. I knew everyone was thinking the same thing as I. I pulled my car over and jumped out. Everyone followed. As I ran to the family plot, it became apparent that the shadow was my mother. She lay between the graves of her husband and her baby. Soaking wet, she appeared lifeless.

"Mom!" I yelled as I ran to her. Henry was on my heels. We both reached her at the same time. Henry checked for a pulse as we dropped to our knees. She was alive at least.

Robert had already dialed 911 on his cell. Henry scooped our mother up into his arms and headed back to the shelter of the car. He laid her down in the back seat of mine.

"Paramedics are on the way," he announced. Mom opened her eyes and looked up at the faces bent over her. "Oh, hi, guys!" She laughed. "It's cold isn't it?" Her teeth chattering.

The sirens blared, coming up the hill. I had my usual, Pavlovian response at the sound of a siren. I always feel as though my chest will explode as I fight back tears. This reaction stemmed from the first of Mother's suicide attempts when the emergency vehicles screamed into our driveway. If I'm stressed, I go right back to that place whenever I hear a siren.

The rain stopped as we watched mother being loaded into the back of the ambulance. Henry climbed in with her for the trip to the hospital. Dwight slipped his hand into mine and squeezed it lightly.

"Do you remember when we all came up here that day to get you Sarah?" Marie asked.

"What are you talking about Marie?" I spun to face her.

"You don't remember?" She looked at me quizzically.

"No. No, I don't," I replied. "I have no idea what you're talking about." I pulled my phone out. "I need to let the girls know we found their grandmother."

Without another word, we all climbed back into our cars and headed for the hospital.

Chapter Nine

Alice Doesn't Live Here Anymore

I did remember. It wasn't something that came to mind often. I had actually blocked the event from memory until therapy brought it back like a gunshot.

I was eleven years old, and raced off the school bus proud of my report card. I had straight A's. My dad wouldn't be home, but I couldn't wait to show mother. How pleased and proud she would be of me. I wanted to see a smile on her face. I never quite knew how I would find my mother. I might find her in a drunken stupor, overdosed, or just comatose, so I always climbed the stairs with trepidation. At the top of the stairs, I saw that she was in her "art room." I swung the door open.

"You are supposed to knock Sarah!" she yelled at me. In front of her was a large canvas she had obviously been working on for a while. The painting was of an adobe style church with arched stained glass windows and a huge wooden door. The sunset sky was painted in blues and pinks. A small child was standing in the foreground. A girl. She wore white and had giant outstretched angel wings. She seemed to be glowing. Her arms stretched toward the heavens. It was Rachel.

"Mom, that's beautiful!" I said in awe.

"Get out Sarah! You should have knocked! Get out of here!" She did not even look back at me.

I felt as if every bone in my body was crumbling. All my internal organs were being drawn and quartered. I took off tearing back down the stairs two at a time. As I grabbed my bike, I dropped my report card onto the pebbles below. I sped down the street, unsure of where I was going. Like a horse that knows where its corral is, my bike seemed to know where I was going. The guard at the gate knew me and let me through. Breathless with tears running down my face, I ascended to Rachel's grave. I dropped my bike and stood before her gravestone.

RACHEL ANNE O'MALLEY
1969-1975
"Our Dearest Angel.
Gone too soon from our arms. Now in God's embrace"

"It's all your fault, Rachel!" I screamed at her headstone. Falling to my knees, I tore at the ground that lay between me and my dead sibling. I ripped up the grass and scooped the dirt below with my hands, frantically trying to reach the box buried deep. I wanted to pull her out of her grave, bone by bone, and take her back to the house, presenting her to mother. "Here, Mom. She's back. Now you can love us all again!"

I hated my sister so much at that moment. If she wasn't already dead, I think I would have killed her. My face was smeared with tears. Every time I tried to wipe them away, the dirt from my hands would make it worse.

I'm not sure how long I had been there before I heard the sirens and vehicles ascending the hill. Someone had called to report seeing a crazed child desecrating a grave site. I considered running. I wished the ground would take me and bury me, too. Someone grabbed me, pulling me off the grave. I was kicking and screaming. I was hysterically out of control. "Let me go!" I screamed.

My father grabbed me. He threw his weight against me and wrapped his arms and legs around me like a giant parental rope. I was finally subdued by his large frame. "It's okay, honey!" he repeated to me until I finally calmed down.

The police left as my father walked me back to the car. They weren't going to prosecute an eleven-year-old. Many people had come up the hill. My father, I later learned, had been in a meeting with Marie's dad when my mother called. I climbed into the back seat of my dad's car and found myself face-to-face with Marie. She looked so dismayed. She didn't know what to say to me. My father thought it a good idea to have Marie try to find me, seeing as she was my best friend. But there we sat, in silence, Marie almost unable to look at me. I resented her for it. I thought no one could possibly understand.

Mother was furious when I got home. I was grounded from everything except school. I didn't really mind. Around that time I discovered books. I immersed myself in reading and escaped into imaginary lands and dreams. My father wanted me to see a psychiatrist. Mother thought the idea was ridiculous. I didn't go. I can see now that it probably would have been an excellent time to begin therapy instead of waiting until my twenties as I did.

Henry had ball practice and various other activities, so the house was fairly quiet in the next couple of months. The "incident" was never brought up again. Mother had planted new flowers and grasses at Rachel's site, so all traces of my violent outburst were gone.

Months later, Henry told me, that he had come home one day and saw mother had built a small bonfire, ostensibly to burn leaves, but he said he saw her throwing different craft items she had made into the fire. Standing close by the funeral pyre was a painting. He said it was of a little girl that looked like an angel. I figured she must have thrown that at the top of the heap as I never saw it again.

When we got to the hospital, Mother was in the emergency room being given IV fluids. Henry conferred with the doctor on call and they decided she should have a chest x-ray. Dr. Dreayer had been called, and he seemed to be on the same page. Her lungs were full of fluid . . . possibly the onset of pneumonia.

Henry and I walked into the little cubicle in the E.R. Her eyes were closed, and she seemed very peaceful. I was certain that this was it for her. Her body was so small and weak, yet only a few weeks earlier she was pretending to jog up and down the street! Henry and I had the inevitable discussion that mother had become a danger to herself. We agreed that I should do what my gut had been telling me all along: to find somewhere safe for her to go. Mother began to stir. She opened her eyes and looked at the two of us. It was apparent that she was confused. "Why am I here?" She asked, looking around the room.

Henry sat on the edge of the bed. "Do you remember going to the cemetery in the rain?"

"No . . . " she answered in a quiet voice.

"Do you know who we are?" I asked.

"Well, of course I do! You're the neighbors!"

After an hour or so, Mother was moved into a room. Marie had called the house again to let the girls know what room number their Grandma was in. Lily said they were on their way. Manuel had already arrived. When I stepped out of Mother's room, I found him standing in the hallway crying. I went over to him and tried to explain what little I knew about her condition and asked if he wanted to see her.

"Of course, Miss Sarah . . . I must see her!" When I led him back into the room, a nurse was checking Mother's blood pressure. She gave Manuel the once over. "You know . . . family are the only ones allowed in Mrs. O'Malley's room."

"This is Manuel." My blood was boiling. "He is family. He is my mother's . . . fiancé." I snapped at her. The nurse looked like she had sucked on a lime.

"Oh well . . . then of course he can stay . . . " she stammered. It was clear what she thought of Manuel.

He looked at me and said quietly, "Thank you." He walked over to my mother's bed and took her hand.

She opened her eyes. "What took you so long?" she asked. They both laughed.

I decided to leave them alone. Seeing the love between them, I resolved to read my Mother and Manuel's writings.

Henry suggested that everyone return to the house. "She shouldn't have too many visitors," he told everyone. "And that includes you, Sarah. I'll wait for Doctor Dreayer and give you all the pertinent information once we have spoken."

Spoken like a true doctor, I thought. "What about Manuel?" I asked.

"Let him stay with Mother for now. I'll bring him home with me later," Henry replied.

In the parking lot, Dwight was leaning up against my car waiting for me. I had forgotten he had been with us. As I approached him, he reached out for me and I fell into his embrace. We stood for a while like that, neither of us talking.

"Want me to drive?" he asked.

"That would be great!"

Chapter Ten

Love In The Time Of La Nina

Summer 1972

We found a small cove. Well, Manny knew where it was. We spread our picnic blanket, and he set out the cheese, bread, and dark purple grapes. We opened a much anticipated bottle of wine that he said he had been saving. I didn't care if it was true or not . . . It was such a sweet thought. I watched how easily this man moved in his skin. He had a confidence that was powerfully attractive to me.

I felt no guilt being with him now. I had left the children at home with their father. I would normally never do anything like that, but ten years had gone by, and I needed to see Manuel again. Sarah was thirteen now and definitely able to handle things should there be a problem. I told Jack I needed time to myself, which was partially true. I hadn't seen Manuel since Rachel's death and since the birth of his children.

We enjoyed our perfect meal. The sun seemed to light up Manny's skin, which was more burnished than I remembered. Even though we had never stopped corresponding and sent photos back and forth, he looked different. He was a man, not a boy anymore. He claimed that he never regretted leaving the church at twenty and that it wasn't until his daughter was born that he realized he was where he was supposed to be . . . being a dad to his kids. His parents had arranged a marriage to a girl Manuel had grown up with. Since he needed to begin a new life he agreed to the marriage. His young wife had died in childbirth with the second baby. He had raised his two very young children on his own. I remember how sad I felt when he wrote to me about his wife.

Not long after consuming our delicious picnic, he suggested going into the water. I had left my suit at the hotel. Manny stood above me and began to slowly take off his clothing. I had only seen two men naked- Jack and Manny. Manuel had become so much more of a man since the last time I had seen him I was surprised upon seeing his defined chest and strong stomach. He said everyone swam naked at this cove. I don't know what possessed me, but I stood up facing Manuel, who had stripped down to his boxers. He began to undress me slowly. Manuel had not seen me naked since the children were born. I knew my body had changed, but I wasn't self-conscious, which surprised me. I was al-

ways concerned about how I looked with Jack. The various women he chose to be involved with were all strikingly beautiful.

We stood naked, staring at one another for several seconds. Manny took my hand, and we both ran for the water. I felt like a school girl laughing all the way to the ocean, which was so much warmer than I had imagined. There was barely a wave in sight. I held onto his neck as we floated and kissed. I had never made love in water, and it was amazing. We made love twice that day, once again on our blanket on the beach as we watched a glorious sunset. I was alive again.

I stared out the plane window. We had hit some turbulence due to the hurricane off the coast. What was I thinking? Flying during a hurricane? I get so nauseated on boats and bumpy planes and pink cars. If I look at a shaken snow globe too long, I want to puke. But here I was on a bumpy plane waving the flight attendant away for the third time. She keeps asking if I'm okay. It must be the puce green color of my face. I closed my eyes and drifted off to sleep.

It was the first time we had traveled together. Although we had been friends for eight or more years we had never taken a trip together. I had been married and divorced, and she had been with her girlfriend for going on two years. But here we were, in the windy city, where it was blistering cold and snowing.

The roll away bed had been moved into a corner of the room as we had requested. It resembled something out of a MASH unit. I sat atop it, feeling the exposed springs under my rear end. The two of us laughed at the absurdity of the situation and agreed we should just sleep in the same bed. Her girlfriend didn't have to know! It was so late, and we were so tired what could possibly happen?

After bustling around unpacking, brushing teeth, washing our faces, getting into our PJ'S we both climbed into the bed. We lay in the dark discussing how we thought the meeting with the television producers would go the next day. Ashley and I had decided to become writing partners a couple of years ago because we made one another laugh a lot and came up with unusual ideas for shows. We finally got a deal on our show "To Hell in a Hand-Basket."

As we lay together, it became more than apparent that both of our bodies began putting out intense heat. I had always been aware of an attraction I had felt for Ashley, but never having been with a woman, I never understood what I was really experiencing. Since she was a gay woman, the flirting we did seemed innocent and maybe even appropriate. But here we were now in a bed, our bodies touching and the steam rising in the air.

"What are you thinking?" Ashley asked in the dark.

"What are YOU thinking?" I threw it back to her.

"I think I need to kiss you!" Ashley said, turning in my direction.

"Good answer," I said, reaching for her mouth with mine.

Her lips were perfectly soft and smooth. It was as if I were kissing a cloud. As our tongues found each other's she plunged hers deeply into my mouth causing my body to shudder. Kissing Ashley was very different from any man I had ever kissed. I was amazed that I wasn't nervous. It felt so natural to be holding this woman in my arms. I lifted her top exposing her voluptuous breast and instinctively pinched her nipples. She arched her back and grabbed my hand moving down between her legs.

"Feel how wet I am," she said, her breath heavy.

I found her exactly as she described. Wet and waiting. But she had plans for me first. Flipping me over onto my back, she lifted my nightgown and began to kiss and lick my stomach. My thighs. My knees. I couldn't stand it anymore and grabbed the back of her head and placed it where I needed her to be.

I had never experienced such intensity before. My body reacted with each kiss, each touch, each flick of her tongue. Her breath was hot and I was on fire.

We made love to one another all night. Taking turns, pleasuring the other. It was as if we both had longed for one another for such a long time. Not knowing how the other felt. Not knowing what crossing that proverbial line would mean to our friendship. But in those few hours of sexual energy and powerful emotions, neither of us cared to look into the future. This was our time, right now. This moment. Two women lost in one another's arms and desires.

I awoke from a large turbulent bump. We began our descent. Reaching over to the seat next to me, and grabbed on to Mother, holding her tight as another bump sent me reeling.

I had promised Mother and Manuel I would bring her to Mexico to him. Fortunately, Henry and the rest of the family supported their wishes. Having read their letters and Mother's journal, it was obvious theirs was a great love story.

Why is it that waiting for your luggage is more stressful than any other moment of travel? Will my bag come down the chute? Will my bag not come down the chute? What if they lost my bag? What did I have in my bag that is really important and will cause terrible angst if I don't get my bag now!? I began concentrating on the teenaged girls in front of me, trying to distract myself from the sick feeling in my stomach. Both were highlighted blondes with great bodies and spray tans. What intrigued me most was the way that they spoke.

"So, he said have a good time, and I'm all, thank you and he's all, but don't have too good a time, like I want you to miss me and I'm like well are you gonna miss me? And he's all like maybe." And then they giggle. Where did the English language go?

Finally the luggage arrived. Remembering that drinking a coke could settle my stomach, I bought a big gulp on the way to find a cab.

It took about forty-five minutes to get to the hotel from the airport. I had never been to this part of Mexico. I loved the vibrant colored tiles that adorned the walls of some of the houses. The hotel was situated on a beach, and I could see even from the lobby that the ocean was crystal clear. The hurricane was a few hundred miles away in the Gulf and was expected to hit within the next couple of days. Although we wouldn't be in the direct path, we would have heavy rains and fairly large wind gusts. Judging from the tourists in the lobby, I was relieved that no one seemed to mind. I was only staying the one night as Manuel lived another hour away. I would be going to take Mother to his home in the morning.

The room was as luxurious as I had expected. In one of the hotels his family owned, Manuel had made all the arrangements. He had been back in Mexico for over a month. Back in California Manuel finally sat down with me and confessed what I pretty much expected. He wasn't really a gardener. He knew that I was aware of everything that had gone on between my mother and him. He spoke of my Mother as if she were an Angel. He knew he would never love anyone as he loved her. From the moment they had met, he knew his life would never be the same. I knew all about their love from all the letters and mother's journal.

June 1953

Dear Diary,

I really didn't want to take this trip. These girls I'm with are loud and giggly. I do like Veronica though. She and I started this school at the same time and didn't know anyone. After Mom died, Dad was transferred to another fire department, and I had to change schools again.

It took us all day on the bus to reach the border. Luckily, I slept most of the way. Jack had come to the house to say goodbye. It was uncomfortable for me. I had tried to tell him I didn't want to see him anymore, but he started to cry! Imagine that. An eighteen-year-old man crying.

Oh well, I suppose we will talk more when I get home.

We will be staying at a hostel tonight after our volunteer work at the orphanage, and then we will head up the coast and spend time on a beach. I am looking forward to that.

I settled into the room quickly, kicking off my shoes to relieve my feet. Once I hit terra firma and gulped the gigantic, cold coke, my nausea had subsided. I reread mother's entry and set the journal down. I ran a bath in the jacuzzi tub and immersed myself for almost an hour. I realized how hungry I had become. Refreshed, I decided to head downstairs. I put the 'do not disturb' sign on the door and made for the bar first.

I love bars. Any kind of bar. Hotel bars, airport bars, dive bars . . . it didn't matter, because they were always a fabulous place to people watch. The more people drank, the more they seemed to relax and reveal themselves. I pulled up a stool and ordered a Margarita on the rocks. Mexico, Tequila? What else would I drink?

I scanned the room and noticed an older couple eating at a two top. They didn't look up from their plates. They weren't speaking at all to one another. It was sad that after many years together, they had run out of things to say. At the other end of the bar, a man sat staring at the flat screen television watching a soccer game while his inebriated date's face was inches away from the granite bar. Sitting a few chairs from me was a young woman, who was constantly applying make-up—obviously a hooker.

I opened my mother's journal again and flipped through it. I had been reading it to her while she was hospitalized in hopes that it would trigger memories and help in her recovery. I don't think a lot of what I had read to her had completely sunk in for me. Rereading her words was like seeing through different eyes this go round. The pages were filled with so many things that I never knew about my parents.

September, 1970

Jack didn't know that I had seen him with Jocelyn. Although I had confronted him about their relationship before, he denied any wrong-doing. Our marriage had reached a point at which I should expect Jack would move from one woman to another. It didn't really matter to me. But Jocelyn? Sarah's best friend's mother? Why would he bring it into our backyard?

I had asked mother about this entry, but she had no recollection about the incident or that she had written this entry. It did make me wonder if Marie may have known about our parents and I debated asking her.

Now that she was happily shacked up with Sybil in a gurus love nest in India, she was impossible to reach.

It wasn't as if I didn't know about my father's propensity toward the opposite sex. Before he died, I forgave him that. The fact that he told me on his death bed that he only loved my Mother calmed the sting . . . and I believed him.

SUMMER 1953

I wasn't sure what to say to Manuel when he asked me to go to the beach alone. We weren't really supposed to leave the group. I had already spent time meeting his parents at their hotel. We agreed that we would meet after everyone went to bed. How scandalous, I thought. Veronica said that she would cover for me . . . whatever that meant, I didn't care. I had huge butterflies in my stomach at the thought of doing something so risky. I couldn't eat supper tonight. What is the worst thing that could happen? If I were caught maybe they would suspend me from school. So what? I am an excellent student . . . I would just say I was influenced by the wonders of what Mexico had to offer!

So I sit here, in the dark, with my flashlight waiting to climb out of my window to the boy waiting below.

What if he doesn't show? I hadn't thought of that. We only met a couple of days ago. What if he changes his mind, and I am standing alone in the dark of night for hours?

What am I doing? What is it about this boy?

After reading Mother's and Manuel's letters and her journal, it was obvious that Mother loved Manuel more than she loved my father. I often wondered how all our lives would have been if Rachel hadn't died. Would mother have crossed that line with Manuel as easily as she did? Would my Father have strayed so much? Losing a child will do one of three things. It will either rip a couple apart, pull them closer together, or they will stay together although they are emotionally apart.

Mother was seventeen when she met Manuel and was already engaged to my father. At eighteen, Manuel planned to dedicate his life to the church. They didn't stand a chance back then. I closed the journal and sipped my drink. I wasn't all that hungry anymore.

I looked around the bar again and noticed the hooker was now talking to a man sitting next to her. She flipped her hair several times and threw her head back as she laughed. The couple I had pitied earlier for their silent meal had finished and were signing to one another. They were deaf! So much for my powers of observation.

As for the other couple, the inebriated woman was still face down on the bar while her date dove into his chips and guacamole, oblivious that she was unconscious.

"Miss Sarah?"

I turned to see a handsome man in a suit and tie. I nodded, and he introduced himself as Michael Hernandez, the general manager of the hotel and Manuel's son.

"Oh! Hello," I said, beginning to stand.

"Please don't get up," he gestured for me to stay on my bar stool. "I wanted to make sure you were here safely and that you have everything you need."

"Everything is perfect, thank you. How's your father?" I asked.

"He is anxious to see you . . . You did bring your mother, no?"

"Of course. I promised."

He took out his business card and handed it to me. "We will drive to my father's home tomorrow morning. It will only take a little under an hour. If you need anything before that, this is my number. You can call me anytime." He handed me the card. As I took it, he kissed the back of my hand gently. "It is good to meet you, at last, Miss Sarah."

I felt my face flush a little. An overwhelming sadness swept over me. Here were two children of two people who had a great love. I wondered if I would ever find such devotion in my life time. I watched Michael walk away and finished the remains of my drink. My stomach was beginning to rumble, so I decided to go back to the room and sleep. It was going to be an emotional day tomorrow. I hadn't seen Manuel for a month, and here I was in his homeland with family members I had only heard about.

The cramps and nausea hit around midnight. I started to sweat profusely and then felt as though I was freezing to death. I began panting like a dog, trying to will away what I knew was about to happen. As I streaked across the hotel floor toward the bathroom, I knew the war inside had won its battle with me. I couldn't understand how it had happened. I was extremely careful. I only drank bottled water on the plane and I kept hand sanitizer on hand at all times. Oh . . . wait . . . the oversized coke with tons of ice. Dammit . . . that was probably it! So much for settling my stomach.

I sat atop the porcelain praying to God to take me now. I have never been so sick. It occurred to me that I wouldn't be able to take Mother tomorrow if I was still feeling this way. I couldn't think of anything else to do. I called Michael.

He was at my door almost immediately. He looked so handsome in his tee shirt and jeans, his hair slightly ruffled from bed covers. My hair was plastered to my face, and I must have looked like an anemic reptile. Michael stepped into the room carrying a plastic bag with miracle pills and bottled water. He sat on my bed and fed me the pills and gave me fresh water. "It will take a couple of hours to work," he said, "but it will work, I promise."

He stayed next to me the rest of the night. I found myself curled up in this stranger's arms, feeling safer than I had ever felt. Mind you, I was delirious and probably would have curled up in Hannibal Lecter's arms just knowing someone was taking care of me. I guess in some ways we weren't really strangers. Both of our parents were so connected I figured Michael and I must be even if by osmosis. I was certainly grateful to have someone taking care of me not just because I was so acutely ill and probably delirious, but because these last few months were traumatic and I had had to deal with most of it alone. It was finally catching up with me.

Chapter Eleven

What Ever Happened To Baby Jane?

Just the names of those places freaked me out. Sunrise Living, Happy Home, Upward Bound. If I was taken to any one of these places, I would know that was it for me just from the names alone. I would know I was a goner. These badly named places came highly recommended by Dr. Dreayer and Mother's attending physician at the hospital. After a week stay, Mother was well enough to come home. I had already been to visit these facilities. The decision we faced was whether she should be kept in the assisted living quarters or with patients suffering from Alzheimer's, or to come home. We unanimously chose the last option.

Tests revealed she was suffering from congestive heart failure, and her cancer had spread. Basically, it was count down time. She seemed lucid in the hospital and was only disoriented a few times. Once home, she withdrew into herself more and more. Everyone else had gone back to his or her own life. Phoebe stayed the longest, but headed back to culinary school the day we checked Mother out of hospital. Terry went with her. He said he wanted to make sure she settled back into her routine. We all knew he was smitten. Brad had wanted to stay, but I insisted he go home and stay out of my hair. Soon after he got home, the house we had shared together sold, and he and Barbie got back together. He assured me that he would handle everything so I could concentrate on taking care of Mother. Lily went back to school, and Henry went home to his patients and family. Dwight was calling almost every day, which was sweet, but I really didn't have a lot to say to him. He mentioned he was going to take a trip, and I encouraged him. All decisions were left up to me and Manuel. Marie and Sybil were meditating in India. Oy vay! I never saw that one coming. All the while, I tried not to feel too alone. Of course I knew I wasn't completely alone. Manuel was still in the rocket ship. It never occurred to him to leave.

After a month at home, Mother's lungs began to fill up with fluid, and she had to be readmitted into the hospital. They drained 12cc's from her chest cavity, a significant amount, I was told. Everything seemed to be going on fast forward. I wasn't sure I could keep up with the waves of emotion. Although I had hoped we could watch her peacefully fade at home, I was much more secure having her in a hospital environment. She had a series of minor strokes that caused her to aspirate. Her body began to fail. A feeding tube was surgically inserted into her stomach. For a woman who attempted so many times to end her life, she now seemed determined to live. She would develop a raging fever and could barely open her eyes or lift her head. I would walk in, and she would look like she wasn't breathing. I was told to prepare myself. Then she would rally. Her fever would disappear, and she would be sitting up watching a soap opera the next time I walked in. Her mind was fading rapidly, which seemed a blessing to me. She wasn't completely aware of all the things shutting down in her body. As always, Manuel was a constant, calming, presence. He was never obtrusive, always careful to put family first. He seemed to know when it was appropriate to give me a breather. I would find him, sitting at her bedside all hours of the day or night, holding her hand or rubbing her forehead.

Sometimes she screamed unintelligible things at imaginary people. She talked of a man in a sweater who would fly around her room or sit on her bed. I wondered if she was seeing my father. Sometimes,

I found myself sitting in the hospital chapel actually praying, which surprised me. I figured it couldn't hurt, and I wanted the final transition to be easy. I had saved her life so often, but I couldn't save her now. Family did trickle in, here and there, but no one stayed very long. It was difficult for everyone to get on planes, or drive such long distances. When they could, they would come even if only for a day. My girls were terrific. We communicated once a day in some form or fashion. I showed up one rainy day to find Manuel already at her side. Mother was in one of her more lucid moments.

"Sarah!" She looked right at me in full recognition, "Do you have any make-up?"

I told her I had a little blush and some lipstick in my bag.

"Let me have it!" she said and held out her hand.

I rummaged quickly through my handbag, finding the items requested, and placed them into her open hand. She looked down at the treasures and smiled like a kid at Christmas. "Make-up!!" She sighed. "Put it on me!"

Make-up for Mother was only applied for special events. She wasn't the kind of lady who wore it every day. A little lipstick was all she used on a daily basis. If she had a special engagement, she would go to the department store and have someone at the make-up counter apply it for her.

Heeding her request, I began applying what make-up I had to her sallow skin. She looked at herself in a mirror I held up for her. She turned her head from side to side, checking out the various angles of her face and smiled. I had sent Manuel down to the shop in the lobby for an eyebrow pencil and nail polish. We played dress up, and she was happy. I painted her fingernails, Manuel did her toes. She was almost all there with us. Then I caught her staring at me

"Are you a part of me?" she asked with her head tilted to the side.

"Yes, Mother . . . I am your daughter . . . Sarah. I am definitely a part of you. And you are a part of me."

She took my hands in hers and kissed them over and over. As if some kind of switch was flipped, her eyes went blank. The woman who was so connected a few seconds ago, slipped away. All expression was totally erased from her face. She lay her body back down on her bed complete with made up face, fingers and toes. She never spoke to either of us again.

I continued to read aloud from different sections of her journal and various correspondences between her and Manuel.

SEPTEMBER 1960

I was totally prepared to tell Jack that I couldn't marry him. I was willing to incur the wrath of my parents even. But I was pregnant. How could I explain that? Jack and I had only kissed. I couldn't even tell Manuel. He was already preaching in the local church. So tomorrow I shall take my vows and marry Jack. I wonder if I will ever experience that kind of excitement for Jack that I had felt in such a brief time with Manny.

Manuel told me that mother had miscarried that baby two weeks after her wedding to my Father. I wondered if that was true, or whether, knowing my mother, if she might have done something to make herself abort. I never got to ask her, but I am sure, it was a blessing it turned out that way.

When I awoke the morning after being so sick, my first night in Mexico, Michael had already left. I felt so much better. Whatever he had given me had allowed me to have a good night's sleep. He left a note saying he would meet me in the lobby at noon, and we would all drive to his father's house together.

We drove with Mother in the back seat. It all felt very strange—as if I was watching myself from above. The trip took a little less than an hour. We drove on a road that overlooked the ocean. Michael pointed out historical landmarks along the way. He spoke about his family. I heard things about Manuel that I never knew. Manuel's parents had emigrated from Spain and had opened a very successful small restaurant, which expanded into a small hotel. The popularity of this quaint seaside vacation spot grew, and they decided to open another. Before long, they had several elegant boutique hotels. They purchased a vineyard and the hotel I had just stayed in. Manuel had married soon after meeting my mother and had children of his own. Michael never knew his mother, but he did know that his father had never stopped loving mine.

We turned off of the main street and headed up a long narrow hill.

"Almost there." Michael said.

A magnificent villa was perched at the top of the hill. This was another piece of his life Manuel had kept to himself. After another sharp curve, we were at imposing iron gates. The wrought iron letters that adorned the gates, read, Vista Linda.

"It means beautiful view." Michael said.

"Indeed."

Michael pushed a code into the box in front of the gate, and the gates swung open. We drove up a tree-lined drive to the beautiful house. Large trellises and arbors were dripping with grapevines that climbed toward the sky. There were horses in a paddock and a small pond peeked out from behind a well-trimmed hedge. I stared in awe at the magnificent Mediterranean home before me.

"Wow. Your father is filled with surprises!"

I saw Michael smile out of the corner of my eye.

"Mom," I said, looking into the back seat. "You are finally back where you wanted to be!"

When the car stopped Manuel appeared at the top of the marble steps that lead to the massive wooden front door. His smile was warm and familiar. Michael got out of the car and opened my door for me, a courtesy I wasn't accustomed to. I reached into the back seat and picked up mother's urn from the box she had been traveling in. I held it tightly as I looked at Manuel. Neither of us spoke as I put the urn into his hands. He looked down at the remains of my mother and smiled again.

"Gracias, Miss Sarah. She is home now."

I knew what he meant.

• • •

It had been a beautiful day. I had gone into mother's garden and cut an array of various flowers to take to her in the hospital. Manuel offered to drive me as I was a little shaky. It wasn't as if I hadn't prepared for this day for several months. I actually think I had prepared my whole life for this day. So many times I had been told to brace myself for my Mother's not coming home. I tried to recall how many actual suicide attempts she had made, but there were too many. Henry had flown in the night before and was already in Mother's room when Manuel and I arrived.

She looked so small in the bed. I felt that in the last week I had actually seen her shrink before my eyes. Once she had stopped talking, everything went fairly fast. Her kidneys began shutting down, and she had suffered a heart attack. I was originally disturbed that the doctors had intubated her, but it all happened so quickly. By the time I got to the hospital, it was too late to do anything. One week later, we were about to make a critical decision.

Manuel, Henry, and I waited just outside her room as the doctor disconnected the life support. We were told she could go at any time or it could take several hours. It didn't matter. We knew we would be there for her, and for us.

I had placed all the beautiful flowers, from her garden, around her room, and we played a variety of her favorite songs that Henry had downloaded onto his iPod.

If I had to describe what it feels like to watch someone die, I'm sure I would not be able to. Although I have spent almost my entire adult life writing about people's feelings and emotions and desires, I can't possibly explain the intense pain that seared through my heart. I kept looking into the faces of my brother and Manuel. Henry had seen many people pass on, of course. Manuel had watched his wife die in childbirth. I had been with my father. But I couldn't register anything unusual in their faces and I wondered if they could in mine.

Mother's breathing was shallow and sporadic. The respirator had kept a constant rhythm forcing her lungs to take in the life force. Now she was on her own.

The breath. The ultimate gift. We take for granted how blessed we are to have it. A breath is the most important thing to happen to every human being. We celebrate the precious moment that a baby takes its first breath. Why do we forget breath's importance until we are about to take our last breath? Watching my parent's taking their own final breaths has only confirmed I must appreciate as many breaths of my own, as I can. Manuel held one of Mother's hands and I the other. Henry sat at the foot of her bed. At exactly twelve noon, she stopped breathing. The song that was playing was Red Sails in the Sunset. It was a song that she and Manuel had their first dance to. I looked over at Manuel and through his tears, I detected a smile.

Her face finally looked at peace. Although I shed many tears, I felt a sense of relief. I hoped that maybe she would find Rachel. I hoped that maybe my father helped her cross over. Being the skeptic that I am, I knew that I might be fooling myself.

Henry and I let Manuel lay with her for a while. Henry and I stood outside her door and wept in each other's arms.

• • •

Mother had asked for some of her ashes to be buried next to my father and Rachel, but she very much wanted to be close to the man she had loved for so long. As I entered Manuel's splendid home, my eyes were immediately drawn to a painting above the mantelpiece, a painting I had thought my mother had destroyed many years before. Little angel Rachel stood before an adobe style chapel, her wings spread, her eyes looking toward heaven. The song "Play that funky music white boy" began in my head, and I was down for the count.

Fortunately, Manuel was aware of my disorder and calmly set me on one of the couches in the living room. Michael, once again, held a wet rag on my forehead. *Déjà vu* all over again. It took a while to get over the surge of powerful feelings spinning in my head.

"When did mother give you that painting?" I asked Manuel, pointing to it.

"I discovered it in the garage a couple of years ago," he replied.

I explained that I thought she had burned it.

Manuel told me that when he discovered it, it had been damaged slightly. When he asked Mother about it, she told him she pulled it out of the fire almost as quickly as she had put it in. She burned other paintings that day, but changed her mind about this one.

"I don't mean to be rude Manuel, but why would she give you a painting of a little girl you never knew?" I asked sitting up.

Manuel held out his hand to me. "I will show you something," he said and took my hand. Michael followed close behind. We walked down a long corridor, passing the formal dining room. A large glass table top sat perched atop a wrought iron base in the shape of a tree. The room was teeming with light that poured in through the massive windows. The kitchen sparkled with industrial steel. A long marble topped island in the middle of the kitchen was surrounded by modern wooden bar stools. I coveted the six burner Wolf stove and copper hood. We stepped out of the back of the house through plantain shuttered French doors. The hills strewn with vineyards were heavy with bursting fruit.

"We are one of the finest wineries," Michael explained.

We walked down one hill and then up several stairs. We climbed the crest, and there was the chapel. The one in my mother's painting. Manuel explained that he had built the Chapel to be closer to God. It was beautiful. We walked up to the front of the church and stood before doors that were made of thick Vermont maple. They were heavy and hard to open. Inside rows of handmade pews, each one slightly different in size and color, filled the small church. The stained glass windows looked as though they were made by children. Innocent, busy, and bursting with too much color. The light streamed through them casting rainbows everywhere in the Chapel.

"Manuel . . . this is beautiful!"

"Si, Miss Sarah, it is home to me."

We walked up to the altar where Manuel and Michael genuflected in front of a beautiful wooden cross. I hadn't been in a church for eons, but I instinctively crossed myself, too. Manuel placed Mother's urn in front of him as he knelt in prayer. The emotion in his voice revealed a lifetime of love and devastating loss and the comfort of eternity. I had a deep understanding right then that I was an orphan. I hadn't processed this yet. I had so many other things to tend to. A lump came up in my throat which I tried to suppress. I had cried privately a few times, and I intended to keep it that way.

We had previously planned to bury my mother's urn in the tiny, family cemetery behind the chapel the next morning. Manuel's mother, father and wife were already buried there. She would be resting next to his wife and a family she never knew. This is what she wanted.

I asked her about this while she was still responsive in the hospital. She replied, "Why is it odd? We all loved Manuel and he loved us!"

Hmmm . . . guess it made some sort of sense to me.

After we all had some private time in the chapel, Manuel mentioned he had planned an early supper. He assumed that I might like to go to my room and freshen up. I was feeling a little overwhelmed. His suggestion was very thoughtful. We walked back toward the house as the sun began to set.

I was introduced to an older woman, Rosa, who was to show me my room. We climbed the marbled staircase. I looked down and saw that Michael was watching me until I got to the landing. He gave me a little wave. I was shown to a large guest bedroom. The room was perfection. Shades of yellow and white splashed the room. Toile curtains hung in heavy cascades. An adobe style fireplace was already burning in the corner, filling the room with the scent of pine and cedar. Rosa had already laid my suitcase neatly on the bed. I thanked her as she excused herself.

I wandered into the bathroom. I am fairly sure that I made an audible noise as I gazed at the bathroom of my dreams, hell, anyone's dreams! Blue slate floors and white porcelain fixtures. The bath tub took center stage in the middle of the room. I assumed what hung from the ceiling was the bath fixture as there were no regular taps on the tub. It perched directly over the center of the bath like a swan's neck. I had never seen anything like it. I had to try it immediately. I turned on the taps, which were positioned on the wall behind the bath, and watched as the water cascaded from the spout like a waterfall. I stripped down. Just as I was about to become the mermaid I had imagined being as a kid, I heard a knock at the door. "Damn!" I pulled one of the oversized, pristine white towels off its rack and scooted back into the bedroom.

Michael was at the door. Seeing me wrapped in a towel, he blushed and apologized profusely. I was nonchalant about it. As I attempted to tuck a stray hair behind my ear my towel slipped, exposing one of my breasts. I re-wrapped myself immediately.

Michael turned his back to me completely mortified, "Miss Sarah, I only wanted to offer a walk before dinner . . . I thought you might like to see the rest of the house and property! I am so sorry to disturb you!"

"It's quite alright, Michael. I was just going to take a bath . . . . Oh no! The bath!" I had left it running . . . . I raced back into the bathroom in the nick of time. The water level had reached the brim. I called out that I would love to take a walk with him. I would meet him in about an hour downstairs.

"Good!" he said, closing the door behind him.

I slipped into the tub. "Awww . . . man! Luxury!"

The grounds were as extraordinary as everything else in Manuel's home. Along the way, a number of various herbs, vegetables, and flowers lined the path. Michael walked me down to the pool where a grand gazebo sat like a sentry overlooking the pool. "This just gets better and better!" I said to Michael, taking it all in.

"Yes, my father is very proud of it all," he replied just as the sky began to rumble.

"Is that thunder?" I asked.

"Yes . . . big storm coming."

And as if on cue, large drops of rain pelted us. He grabbed my hand and we bolted for cover in the gazebo. Sheltered under the gazebo roof, we watched the deluge. There was no warning. We were stranded and quite far from the house.

"I will call the house, so they can bring us umbrellas," Michael said, reading my mind. "It should only be a few minutes. The gazebo will keep us dry until then."

"Ok, just don't start singing, 'I am sixteen going on seventeen.'"

He looked at me blankly. "I don't know what you are referring to, Miss Sarah."

"Never mind . . . it wasn't that funny!"

Taking his coat off, Michael wrapped my shoulders with it, then he made the call to the house. It didn't take long before the troops arrived, Manuel among them. Even with oversized umbrellas, we were still soaked by the time we got back inside the house.

I changed my clothes for the third time that day.

We were supposed to have dinner in the stately dining room, but I suggested it might be more intimate in the kitchen at the cozy banquette. As everything else about Vista Linda, the meal was flawless. Manuel was thoughtful as we enjoyed his famous tamales with Spanish rice and sangria. It seemed a good time to ask Manuel to tell the story of how he had actually met and fallen in love with Mother.

He took a deep breath before beginning. "I was running to catch the bus that was to take me to my parents' hotel after school, because I was late. The driver stopped when he saw me, so I could board. My breath was heavy as I got on the bus. I felt like I could collapse. I heard the sounds of girls laughing. I found a seat next to an old lady.

"When I looked across the aisle I saw a young girl reading a book. There were a lot of girls on the bus, and they seemed to be together. The one across from me wasn't paying attention to the others, so I thought maybe she wasn't with them. She was very pretty.

"She had beautiful blonde hair and large eyes. I could tell even though she hadn't looked up from her book. The next stop was mine, so I got up. The girls did too, except for the one reading. Someone called "Olivia, we have to get off now." She put down her book, and I saw that she was with these girls. I let her go before me, and she thanked me. I looked into her eyes, and I wanted to talk to her, but she got off very fast.

"All the girls walked down the street toward the market place. I was supposed to go the other way, but I wanted to talk to this girl, so I followed them. When we got to the market, all the girls went different places, except for Olivia who sat down on a bench to read her book. I watched her for long time. She must love this book, I thought.

"I finally went to her and sat with her. My English wasn't that good, but I told her that I saw her on the bus. She didn't want to talk. I asked why she didn't go with her friends. She said that she didn't like to do tourist things. She explained that they were on school trip. I suggested that I take her to places not for tourists. She was uncomfortable. I invited her to come see my parents at their hotel first. She agreed and told a friend she would be back at their hotel for dinner. We walked for a while and talked. I had never met so smart a young girl."

He paused. He was fighting tears. Manuel went on to describe Mother meeting his parents. He took her to one of the beaches that the locals frequented. For the next three days, he showed her what she never would have experienced as a tourist. "In such a short time we felt things so fast." He sighed.

I asked him if he could elaborate a bit more providing it wasn't too difficult.

"How does one explain how the earth moves around the sun? How each star winks back at us when night falls. That each drop of rain is full of the ocean, and the ocean is full of the rain? I cannot explain in words how my heart was captured by this girl. Olivia said we had been together in another life, and we found each other in this life too late."

It was clear to him that she had to go back home. She was already engaged to my father. Manuel was going to preach the word of God. Both had lives far away from the other and they were too young or maybe too scared to change their intended destinies.

As I learned in the journal, Mother had become pregnant at this time. I asked Manuel about that.

"I found out much later about that. We had one night together. Neither one of us had been with anyone before. But Olivia knew that she had to make everything right, so she proceeded to plan the wedding to your father. There was no other decision to be made in those years."

They continued to write to one another. She decided to come back again the next summer . . . which she did. They formed an undying bond that summer that lasted for fifty years!

I was beginning to get tipsy. My glass of Sangria kept being topped off and I just kept drinking. The storm was relentless outside with huge thunder claps and piercingly bright lightning. I was so riveted by Manuel's story I barely noticed.

Mother and Manuel were forever bonded by love and loss in their lives. He told me that Rachel and his wife had died around the same time. The losses had only made their hearts stronger.

When Manuel suggested we all retire, I began thinking about being alone, in a strange house, in a strange bed with my strangely vivid imagination. As I weaved my way up the stairs to my bedroom Michael asked if I would like some tea or if I required anything before he went to bed. I turned to see him looking up at me. "I could use some company, I think." I surprised myself with such boldness. I wondered if it was taboo to sleep with your mother's lover's son?

The sangria had gone to my head. The thunder was growling outside and there would be a lovely fire burning in my bedroom. It was too tempting to resist.

We lay on large pillows in front of the fire sipping tea and talking. I asked him when he first learned of my mother. He said that his father had always spoken of a great love, but had always believed nothing would ever come of it as she was married and lived a long way away. It wasn't until after my father had passed that Manuel told his kids he would go to the U.S. to be with this lady.

"We were very surprised," Michael said, "but because he had spent so many years alone, and because we were grown, I supported him."

"What about your sister? How did she feel?"

"At first she felt that our father was betraying our mother in some way. But our father had never sought out other female companionship, and eventually my sister, Clare, understood."

I hadn't really processed Clare's side of things. After all, Olivia O'Malley had betrayed us too.

"Your mother lost a child and my father a wife. Family dynamics have to change, no?"

I agreed. I liked the way this man spoke. I liked how sympathetic and kind he seemed. Hat's off to Manuel for being a terrific dad.

"We had always wanted our father to be happy. He was so dedicated to me and to Clare. It was harder for her, I think, being a girl and losing a mother so early. I never knew our mother, so it was different for me."

"Where is your sister now?" I asked

"She arrived yesterday and will drive here in the morning to meet you. She lives in Los Angeles now with her husband and two children."

"I see."

I was dying to ask him about his personal life. Was he married? Was there a girl friend? A boyfriend?

"What about you, Michael?" I felt odd. Here we were lying so close to one another, and I didn't really know anything about him.

"I am not married. I was engaged a couple of years ago to a sweet girl. I realized I wasn't in love with her. Another lesson I learned from my father, I suppose. So I broke it off. It wasn't fair to her . . . or to me!"

Secretly, I was relieved at his answer.

"Did your father know that my mother was ill when he went to her?" I brought the topic back around.

"Olivia had told him of her diagnosis when he arrived. It became even clearer to him that he needed to stay."

We spent some time in silence, staring at the fire. Michael got up and put another log on.

I was scheduled to leave the next morning, but the unrelenting storm outside made it easy to decide that I should stay another day or two. Michael suggested that he would cancel my flight for me and arrange for another one. He grabbed the empty tea cups and wished me a better night's sleep than the previous one.

I stood, and we faced one another. Until that point I hadn't noticed that his eyes were actually bright green. Standing so close and looking deeply into them, I thought they were about the most beautiful set I'd seen. I could tell that he was looking deeply into mine as well.

"Thank you for making this day a little more bearable. It is hard enough burying my mother once, let alone twice."

Michael nodded. He understood.

There was an awkward pause as I felt an impulse to kiss him. Instead, Michael bowed his head and bid me good night. I watched him close the door behind him.

Looking around this gorgeous room, I realized how incredibly tired I was. I pulled back the lush eiderdown covering the bed and thought I would just lie down for a bit. The bed was so welcoming. I sunk into it like a contented, well-fed puppy.

I awoke the next morning, still fully clothed, having had one of the best night's sleep in ages. The rain continued pounding away at my windows.

Another burial, on another rainy day. What is it with rain and funerals in this family?

I realized I didn't have much time before we were to lay Mother to rest. So I jumped into the shower and washed my hair quickly.

Rosa met me at the bottom of the stairs with a cup of coffee. She asked me what I would like for breakfast. When I learned that everyone was in the Chapel I wanted to make my way there right away. Grabbing one of the huge umbrellas I headed to the church.

Manuel smiled as I blew into the Chapel. Michael came over to me and helped me with my umbrella. A pretty woman walked over to us.

"Sarah, this is my sister Clare," Michael said.

"I wanted to be here, too," she said, extending her hand to me.

"Thank you," I said, overwhelmed.

It was a short ceremony, partly because of the rain. Manuel said it was the angels crying. I smiled to myself. That was what I had thought the first time I saw mother cry. I believe he knew that somehow.

We left Manuel alone to put mother's ashes in the tiny plot he had prepared behind the church. Michael, Clare, and I raced back up to the house. Michael reminded me that a hurricane was off the coast.

Rosa had a large pot of Colombian coffee brewing and had put out freshly cut fruit and yogurt. We all sat around the table in the kitchen and dug in.

Clare was quiet at first, but when I asked her about her children she became more animated. "My youngest daughter just began college, and my son is a junior partner in their father's law firm. They are wonderful children," she said smiling.

She asked about mine, and I boasted about my beautiful girls. Michael sat quietly, but I could feel his satisfaction that Clare and I were getting along.

"I wanted to let you know that I was able to make another flight for you tomorrow afternoon. The rain is supposed to completely stop by then, and it would be my pleasure to take you to the airport," Michael said.

I thanked him and told him how much I appreciated everything.

Clare was going back to her friend's home about a mile away, but she said she would love to stay in touch once back in California.

"I would love that," I said. I'm sure Mother would have loved it, too.

Back in my room, I sent a couple of e-mails to the girls letting them know I was staying an extra day. Rosa had already tidied my beautiful room and lit another small fire. I considered climbing back into the wonderful bed, but I noticed the rain had subsided quite a bit. Although it was very gray and foggy outside, I thought I might explore the grounds of Manuel's home.

As bundled up as I was, I was having trouble keeping my teeth from chattering outside. I made my way up to the paddock I had noticed on the drive up. Fortunately Rosa had given me an extra pair of Wellington boots. I walked into the stable where the horses were in individual stalls.

Manuel had three mares and a gelding. The male was a gorgeous palomino, the kind of horse that appeared on the cover of one of my books. As I got closer, their ears pricked up and they all blew steam from their noses.

"Hi, guys!" I reached for a couple of apples in a barrel next to one of the stalls. I hadn't been around horses in a very long time, but had always loved them. My father had promised that I might have a pony of my own one day, but after Rachel died I think he had forgotten.

"You like horses, I see?"

Startled, I turned to find Michael standing in the doorway to the stable.

"Yes. I was just thinking how I missed being around them. My father used to take us to the pony rides. As I got a bit older I was allowed to help brush and saddle some of them."

Michael walked over to me. "Want to ride one?"

"Now?" I asked nervously.

"Why not?"

It took about twenty minutes for Michael to saddle up two of the horses. I was actually a bit frightened as I mounted one of the mares. It is very apparent when you sit on top of an equine of the immense power this animal has, and the potential to cause bodily harm to us lowly humans. Michael assured me that Sophie, my horse, was very sweet and calm. Michael looked more than handsome on the Palomino.

I followed close behind as we rode on the trails around the property. The air was crisp and fresh. I had to pull my scarf up over my nose and mouth to keep my face from freezing off. It was exhilarating.

The horses seemed happy to be out. As we trotted up a crest they both became excited. We got to the top of the hill overlooking the valley below and the ocean.

"Beautiful, no?" Michael asked, looking back at me.

All I could do was nod. I was speechless.

He dismounted his horse and came over to mine. He extended his hand, I climbed off Sophie. We stood next to one another staring out at the vista. I realized we were holding hands.

"I can't believe she's gone!" I said out loud.

Michael turned to face me and without warning I began to cry. Slightly at first, but as he wrapped his arms around me, I couldn't control it anymore. The floodgates opened, and I sobbed. I wailed, I made noises I had never made before and my knees grew weak. Michael was steadfast in holding me up. He let my body contort and do whatever it needed to in those moments without saying a word. I hadn't realized how much I had been holding in for so long. I had been so angry at my mother for most of my life, and now that she was gone I didn't know what I would do without her.

Michael insisted I go back into the house to get warm while he took the horses back into the stable. Neither of us spoke on the ride back. I felt as if I had been hit by a bus. I had cried for at least twenty minutes. Walking back, I wondered if I had been selfish with my emotional breakdown. I had lost my mother, yes, but at least I had her for most of my life. Michael had never known his. I hoped I didn't appear to be totally self-involved.

I ventured back toward the chapel before returning to the house. I walked around the back to the tiny cemetery. I could see the small mound of fresh soil just above the existing headstones. Manuel's parents and wife were there, and now my mother was behind them. Manuel had a lovely headstone prepared before we got here. It read:

Olivia Mancuso O'Malley
1942-2012
Mother, Wife, Companion, and loving Friend
May the Angels look upon you forever.

Michael made the most wonderful supper that evening. A Spanish Paella and a lovely salad. He cooks too!

Manuel was very quiet as we sat and ate. But Michael and I couldn't stop talking. I felt a deep sense of relief and release that night. Crying had been cathartic and now that all of Mother's wishes had been granted, I started to feel more like myself again.

Later, Michael and I found ourselves, once again, in my room with another roaring fire and a lovely bottle of wine.

He made love sweetly. It was soft and considerate. His body was firm, and his arms welcoming. He told me how beautiful he thought I was from the moment he saw me. I told him how smart he was . . . and we laughed.

There was a peacefulness lying with him. There was also a sense of sadness. For me, anyway. I liked this man. I hadn't really felt a soul connection like this is a very long time, and I had no idea if I would ever see him again. How ironic, I thought. We were years older than our parents were, but here we were, like them before us. Feeling deep emotions and both of us knowing I would have to leave, and both of us knowing we would have to go back to our daily lives again.

We got to the airport on time, but my plane was delayed. Michael sat with me before I had to go through security. I had left Mother's and Manuel's journal and letters on the table in the foyer for Michael to read. I thought he and Clare might like to understand their father a little better. We sat not saying anything about the previous night together. We were both feeling raw and vulnerable.

My plane was announced and Michael slipped his hand into mine. "I hope this isn't the last time I see you."

I kissed him lightly, and told him I had hoped so, too.

• • •

A year passed by so quickly. I had decided to stay in my mother's home. All the imaginary cobwebs had been removed, and I had a sense of belonging there. Something I hadn't felt in many years. It was also the perfect house for Phoebe and Terry's wedding.

Brad walked her down the aisle and although he brought Witchy Poo along, I was actually okay with it. The only thing Brad and I shared were our children, and we were devoted to making it as easy on them as possible.

Phoebe looked radiant. She was not only beaming about her wedding, but she also graduated culinary school and landed a job as the sous chef in one of the top hotels in San Francisco.

Marie cried on Sybil's shoulder as her brother recited vows he wrote himself.

She and Sybil were planning on buying a home together in Los Angeles. Marie's kids still couldn't accept their mother's new choice of lifestyle and remained back east.

Lily had brought her new love. Another med student, an African American named Omar. Dwight was supposed to attend, but he and Violet were expecting their first baby any day. WHAT EVER HAP-

PENED TO BABY JANE? Manuel had flown here a week before the ceremony and planted all new flowers in Olivia's Garden. The arbor dripped with wisteria and was the backdrop for the exchange of vows. Manuel presided over the communion.

I had kept Manuel's spaceship in the yard and made it my new office. As the kids exchanged their "I do's" the sun changed angles and rays bounced off the Airstream shining a beam of light onto the newlyweds.

"Olivia is giving her blessing!" Manuel said, looking toward the heavens.

I believed that she was.

All in all, I was feeling pretty terrific about my life. *Tequila Sunrise Nights* did what everyone expected and flew off the shelves. It was being made into a movie.

I had finally decided to take the trip to the one place I had wanted to see my entire life. I was going to Africa for an entire month. I had also decided I would try my hand at a "legitimate" novel.

Chapter Twelve

As I waited in yet another airplane terminal, the love of my life who seems to chronically run late, finally appeared out of breath and carrying too may bags.

"Is this running late thing, something I'm going to have to get used to?"

"Yes," Michael said, grabbing me and pulling me to him. "It's all about the moment, dear heart. This . . . right here . . . right now." He kissed me full on the mouth.

A kiss that still sends me reeling.

"I love you now . . . and forever!"

. . .

Chapter One
Home Of The Brave
It's funny that it hadn't occurred to me
until that very moment, when I pulled into my
mother's driveway, that the idea of losing her
would devastate me more than I ever could have
imagined . . . .